Jellybeaners

A Novel By

GENE SCOTT

JELLYBEANERS
First Edition
Copyright © 2017 Gene Scott
All rights reserved.
Edited by Vince Dickinson and Zee Monodee
Published by Alarice Multimedia, LLC.
Cover by Jeffrey Kosh Graphics

ISBN-10: 0692848800
ISBN-13: 978-0692848807

Dedicated to the brave health care professionals scattered across America who – after swearing to do no harm – deny themselves the many perks and privileges offered by the pharmaceutical industry and prescribe opioids responsibly.

Acknowledgements

Many people contributed to the creation of this novel, including early readers Brad Simpson, Kathy Feagins, Connie Hahne, and my first teacher, Kaye Scott.

Editors Vince Dickinson and Zee Monodee burnished the edges and adjusted the focus while family and friends supplied constant encouragement.

And thanks to the love of my life, Lana, whose patience and grace endure.

JELLYBEANERS

GENE SCOTT

2017

Dear Kelly,

Thanks for teaching, and
sharing your love of books!

MB

Kituwah Falls

The bent, rundown shack, patched and cobbled with gray pieces of crating and splintering brown pallet board, windows covered with ripped opaque plastic, squats in a heap off Stout Street, coal smoke twisting out its chimney like vapor from an ebony nostril.

Three children wail hysterically, run in circles, pull their hair, and scream at their father, resting on his knees beside the dilapidated rust-brown '92 Plymouth Horizon, the driver's door flung open.

A school bus squeaks to a halt and four children bounce off, stop in their tracks, and stare open-mouthed at the scene.

Vane Sarge Walker pulls up in his beat-brown 2001 Chevrolet pickup. A trained emergency medical technician, volunteer firefighter, long-retired military serviceman, and recently retired Forest Service ranger, he lives nearby on a fourth-generation family farm.

The Mount Vernon Volunteer Fire Department's red-light-flashing, chartreuse EMS vehicle approaches, the wail of its siren whining faintly, building in slow crescendo as it roars down the twisting mountain valley cut by the ancient Tellico River, which falls down the mountain grade toward the village of Kituwah Falls.

The dirt driveway, strewn with clinkers—cindery particulate chunks of burnt coal dragged out of the leaky furnace and tossed into the potholed driveway—steal Sarge's attention.

A homemade doll mother Sizer crafted and gifted her three-year-old Ashley the previous Christmas sits with its broken neck propped against the largest clinker, the head mashed flat.

Jumping out of his pickup, Sarge purposefully fixates on the doll, briefly ignoring the cacophony, takes a few seconds to collect his wits, and then slowly turns to face the inevitable.

The toy's face, black-button eyes fixed on eternity, glistens wet-red in the short March dusk, staring directly into a gunmetal sky. A dirty-black tire track ends at its chin.

Sarge can neither swallow the sob nor fight back the wave of salt water cascading down the stubble on his cheeks before he turns to face the disemboweled heap lying in the driveway beside the driver, wrapping, then unwrapping his arms across his chest, choking between screams.

Poor Ashley. One more notch on the pill mill tree of shame, thought Sarge.

This couldn't go on. Someone had to put a stop to this…

We're going to pull those sonsabitches out by the roots, come Memorial Day.

Studying a raven circling high over the ridgeline to the east, he swore to himself:

Or die trying.

Samantha Walker's Journal

Dear Mr. Stephens,

I reckon you're my primary audience, since you assigned this journal. Threatening Bo Wruck with death was simply a warning to keep him from wrecking me again, like he did back in October, but my known rifle skills put some meat on the ultimatum.

I'll fulfill your contract and stay out of jail. Anyway, it would set a bad precedent for the valedictorian of Kituwah Falls High School class of 2016 to deliver the graduation-day address holding a wireless microphone in a prison video feed.

But I also want to address my future kids from this journal, should I have any. You never know. I can't really get my mind around this assignment unless I picture an audience. Sorry. It's not that you're not enough of an audience, but you get it, don't you?

You said you'd burn our journals at the end of the semester, Mr. Stephens. But keep mine. I'll hide it at home in case there's any self-incrimination, or any fingers pointing at Bo or Leeza's gang. No one will be able to find this until I'm gone, or until it doesn't matter anymore. I promise.

So, here goes, kiddies. You're not even sexed, yet. Just tiny little bitty microscopic eggs, semi-human, collecting dust. Not much dust, as I'm only 18. Not yet in the prime of reproduction age. Not yet in the prime of anything, really. Yet, so much has happened already, my babies. So much…

***

My life so far has been a full-blown, nature-based, high-definition, enhanced surround-sound, motorcycle-injected highlight-reel for a long stretch. A Disney childhood city folks would find impossible to fathom.

But wondrous rides come to a natural end, sadly. They tell you there's a happy ending. Well, maybe when you're 90 and senile in an old folk's home, then you do get that blissful state of looking back at your life with nostalgia. But all in all, it's a lie. Nothing but a lie... Life, they tell you, is supposed to be happy.

It's not.

And maybe if you're part of the popular crowd, then your life will be different from mine. Never being part of the popular pack has its advantages. Like, I was always gangly. The ugly duckling, tallest kid in the class, pimple-prone. Good luck making Miss Popular with that giraffe look. Not to mention the teasing, asking me what the weather was like in the clouds up there. Makes me want to spit and say *it's raining.* You develop a thick skin this way. And you see things, stuff others don't want you to see, but you do. Again, maybe because you're staring down from that high in the sky. Thankfully, some of the boys caught up in high school, both in size and pimple production. Nerdish. Love that science, which is perhaps a direct link to the Cherokee genes. Natural science. Being in touch with the elements and all that, like my Native culture asks of me. There was that connection, you know.

Then, in the middle of my junior year at Kituwah Falls High School, my body started to blossom. Buh-bye, ugly duckling, hello, um, swan? I wouldn't quite put it like that. I'd already been shaped by that point, not someone to bow along to the crowd.

Mix that reality with my already aggressive, take no prisoners, double back flip off the chicken house, wheelie-for-days, crack rifle shot, straight-A student, type-A Alpha-Woman attitude... and you get Trouble with a capital T.

And that caught the eye of some people. Well, one in particular. And I really couldn't be happier, you know.

Jasper Whitlock—the tall-handsome-sandy-haired-math-brilliant-boy-next-door. We both enjoyed long, slow rides up and down the glorious Cherohala Skyway, mountain breezes pleasuring our skin as we glide through diamond flicker maple forests along the twisting highway, throttle light in the gloved hand. Or the Tail of the Dragon—that world famous Tennessee twister—US 129—sporting 318 curves in eleven miles. A parallel asphalt universe, a death-trap, but not ours; available, but shunned; a pariah, our Tellico River and Fontana Lake and Trans-America Trail and the vast Cherokee National Forest, where buffalo once roamed, fat on windfall chestnuts. Where ancients prospered so long ago, now dwindled to a few dozen, driven into the mountains or down a path of starvation, but genetically linked to the Walkers through the ages, completing my soul and making me eternally connected to the natural world.

Long before the Jackson Death March, aka the Trail of Tears, the bitter slog to Oklahoma, that dusty-polluted-oil-pipeline-fracking-prairie-square of a crud hole.

Don't get me wrong.

I hold nothing against the people of Oklahoma. How could I? Many remain related to me through Cherokee blood. Kituwah (GID-ah-wah. That's how you pronounce it, in case you didn't know. Is the place still standing in your time? Does it still exist?).

But you have to understand something, my babies. I'll tell you it all went to Hell in a handbasket. Bear with me, my younglings.

The government told Oklahomans, Kansans, and Texans to plow up the land following the Homestead Act of 1862, told them "the rain would follow the plow," and told them to replace prairie grass with wheat, kill the buffalo, who flourish from minus 70 Fahrenheit to plus 110, replace them with cattle, which only survive from 0 to 90 Fahrenheit.

So they did.

They shot nearly all the buffalo, leaving most to rot on the ground, and turned the prairie over with Charles Newbold's cast iron contraption.

When the winds blew, the plow-raped prairie dust drifted east across America—residents of Jamaica actually found themselves covered in Oklahoma prairie dust—during the 1930's. Wheat prices fell, and cattle flopped and turned stiff on the desiccated plain. The government quickly issued reports that the settlers were fools to plow up the prairie in the first place.

See where that gets us? Listen to the government, then hear the government say you are an idiot for listening to the government. Repeat this process generation after generation, and you are up to date with 2016:

ISIS terrorism filling the holes of security we left behind in Iraq, after we listened to the government say Iraq held weapons-of-mass-destruction... Listen to the wonderful news that there is no end to the natural gas underground here at home, so fracking it is... and that now causes earthquakes in, guess where? Oklahoma... Hearing from the government that we need genetically modified organisms in the pantry, as these are *better* crops, built to withstand just about anything, excluding a nuclear bomb going off... and then overgrazing pastures to fill the gut of the 39% of US adults that are morbidly obese, with salmonella, E coli, shigellosis, listeria and staph-infected meat.

Ooh, that sounds good!

Hearing we need yet one more rapine oil pipeline strung across the land. Agriculture and cities sucking down the water table as fast as possible. Subsidized farmers taking corn off the table to make fuel that sucks fresh water at an ever-faster rate. California in deep drought, on the verge of collapse, our truck-farmed vegetables dying on the vine... while a chemically-sprayed-orange-faced-politician-wannabe tells us there *is* no drought, whatever we want to hear, truth be damned. He wants the job, make Americans *hate* again. We're going down the pit, my babies. Can you see it, yet?

The old white man won't go up on his roof and nail a shingle. "Bad knees," he says; needs oxycodone every day—pass the bottle, *rattle rattle*—watching Mexicans do the job, but hating Mexicans for taking jobs.

The old white woman loves watermelon and tomatoes and sweet corn, but won't stoop to pick one off the vine. Let the dirty Mexicans do that from dawn to dusk, then hate them for their work ethic—they stole my job, bastards. Not that the old white woman would ever work from dawn to dusk roofing the house or picking the vegetables, craziness running more rampant each day in the Big Pharma-pushed opiate-jangled and alcoholic mind.

One-third of the nation disgruntled, on the couch, listening to news tailor-made to enrage their hearts. This is 2016, my unborn children. You want happiness? There's more than a pill for that. There's one such tablet for everything, actually. And believe me—you'd need that to live in my world.

Silent Colorado mine holes, full of poison, breaking loose and rushing onto what remains of the Navajo. Greedy Wall Street crashing the economy and receiving a bail out, *too big to fail*, while wages for the middle-class remain at 1970 levels—pass the Lortabs, wash them down with Colt 45.

Damn Guatemalan children running from gang warfare and wanting freedom—show me a ten-foot wall, and I'll show you an eleven-foot ladder. The hordes are coming! The hordes are coming, and not *"winter is coming,"* as in this story we all know in my time where, would you believe it, there actually is a wall to keep out the unwanted!

But this state of affairs, everything it's all become—it's much more than an 18-year-old needs to think about, and I don't, really. So why am I running my pen off in these pages, huh? Well, it's fun to write about it all in this journal. It all just pours out, you know. I can get all worked up and run my mouth endlessly, and no one cares. Maybe you, Mr. Stephens, but perhaps not even you in the future, little ones.

Wait a sec, *hello*? If there *is* a future. Why should I spend time thinking about what the *grown-ups* screw up on a daily basis?

They tell me I am the future. That my peers and I are the ones with the keys to tomorrow, that we're the ones who will make America great again.

Pfft. Can you see me laughing my ass off here?

My generation will probably screw it up worse. In wanting to do better, we'll aim higher... into the darkest mess ever to try to cover up the crap of those who came before us. Not worth getting worked up about, really. I reckon every generation thought their elders were screw-ups. You, in the future, know the truth of that, I bet.

But enough of the future, of which I am totally clueless. Let's come back to what I actually know. Right now, I must think about grades, college, and motocross. Do you even know what that is, in your time? Do you kids even get out of the house and go on vehicles and other stuff, or is the world finally fully virtual?

Anyway, motocross helps me blow off steam, so it's necessary. It's my release valve, children. If all the crap inside me bottles up, I get into trouble. That's why I'm scribbling here today. Bo Wruck broke my collarbone last October, and I let myself get bottled up. It ended in a death threat. I chose this journal and counseling over jail. Had a good record, so they let it slide. Bo never got caught with his shenanigans, so he's scribbling, too. Nearly dashed my brains out against that poplar tree, but he's simply scribbling like me.

However...

Mr. Stephens teaches history, and history teaches that we'll repeat the same mistakes if we don't pay attention. And the longer we sleep, or zombie-out-on-electronics, or suck opiates, or down power drinks while flopped on the couch and remain self-deluded and brain-fuzzed-on-sugar—pass those Chips Ahoy and another beer, please—the more difficult it will be to fix the mess. The diabetes. Lines lengthening near dialysis machines. Cancers of every organ proliferating like, well, a cancer. Bigger, heavier scales, so we don't crunch the little ones made for lighter generations.

Dilemma. Who has time for such lofty questions, and frankly, who cares? Being 18 and having to care about the history of bullshit-I-didn't-create. I just want to be 18 and enjoy Jasper, motocross, hunting, fishing, kayaking, and riding the Cherohala. I want peace, my version of it, and screw the rest of the world and all their crap that makes it such a disgusting place. I don't want to think about all this…

But what if I have kids who'll read this in an even crappier world I never attempted to improve? Big dilemma.

Twice, the government told Americans to be patriotic, line up, and charge German machine gun emplacements while breathing mustard gas (WW1) or ducking whistling V-2 rockets (WW2).

Congress promised $500 per man, before the first conflict began, to attack those Germans—kill them all!

However, when Doughboys returned to America sick with the flu, they infected millions of loved ones unintentionally. Thousands died. War might not have come to our shores, but the Grim Reaper tagged along for a ride, anyway.

Then the US government attacked their own so-called *Bonus Army* with fixed bayonets and tear gas—Patton and McArthur's troops did this—as the repatriated troops camped in Washington, waiting for the promised cash to feed their starving families.

Don't believe it? Google *Bonus Army* and see what pops up. Google must be your lifeline in your age. Or do you have a Siri popping up everywhere in a truly globalized world now?

Two or three generations later, the government advises us to frack the land. They even subsidize the effort... then say we are idiots for listening and ruining the ground water with chemicals.

I can see it coming: leaders endlessly repeating the mistakes of the past—a never-ending cycle that perpetuates itself. No wonder schools from sea-to-globally-warmed-sea stopped teaching civics. Who needs morals or a code of ethics when the goal is to destroy by all means and cover our asses whenever any mistake—and trust me, there will be many—is made? And now, the Tennessee legislature is debating whether or not to strip all textbooks of Middle Eastern history and Arab culture. That's a world too fraught with conflict, with radicalism, a world too tainted by all things bad, so we cannot allow it to contaminate the pure minds of our kids. Ha! Do you think they know that algebra, coffee, and mint juleps are Middle Eastern inventions? Mint juleps!

Can you hear yourself lecturing, Mr. Stephens? You taught me all this. Made me look it up through verifiable sources and cross-reference, so I'd know it was true. No wonder you can't get the Yankee stigma out of your name around Kituwah Falls, even though you've lived here 30 years. Really teaching American history! Shameful. Yankee bastard.

Can you hear me giggle here? One of the benefits of journaling is that you can cuss, which I can't at home. Sarge would whip me in a heartbeat. Sorry about that, kiddies. I'll be moldering in the grave, and you'll be looking at pictures of a gray-haired, slope-shouldered hag when you read this.

If I get to that age, mind you. Nothing's ever guaranteed in our times.

Is this rambling now also an ode? To my Cherokee forefathers-mothers-brothers-sisters cast out of Eden, bitch-slapped and driven from Shangri La, turning back to throw one more glance upon running streams, plentiful game, tilled ground, herds of buffalo, strong enemies to test their mettle, but not so powerful that you and yours are annihilated. A wave of human white rats jumping off ships by the tens-of-thousands, gobbling up the land and maiming it beyond repair—New Jersey, Oklahoma—and coming to a head via Andrew Jackson, a talking head, often drunk, shock of white hair, red-eyed and swaggering precursor to Hitler, teaching the finer advantages of concentration camps—a patent Jackson never registered, but the idea his funny-mustachioed German protégé perfected, made factory-efficient. Jewish slave labor handmade each V2 rocket, forced to indirectly kill before they themselves were snuffed out by the thousands in those gas chambers.

Dark, indeed, these angry thoughts, but you're requiring that I write them down, no matter that my style is a crazed Jack-Kerouac-cacophony of pissed-off-ness.

Mrs. Johnson, our beloved English teacher, assigned Kerouac, *Dharma Bums*, *On the Road*, *The Town and the Country*—my favorite—and now I find myself in a stream-of-consciousness phase, blubbering down personal stuff here on this stay-out-of-the-jailhouse paper in a rushing see-smell-hear-taste-feel-everything way. Kerouacian cussedness.

But when you're pissed, it's best to lay it all out there, screw it, beating the bed with the tennis racket, take your dad's old Colt .45 service piece out to the back yard, set up a dozen glass jugs—or better yet, an old washing machine, a dog-turd dead computer, a printer forever leaking ink all over your hands, some kind of man-made-pain-in-the-ass machine begging to get blown to smithereens... and then don't you just love the physicality of those rounds popping off in your hand, smoke flying, parts scattering across the yard like so many limbs torn off a beast? So cathartic. No need to poison yourself on drinks or drugs; you actually need a physical release, like riding motocross, cross-country running, and sex (I assume).

sigh

Sam Walker, 18 and still a virgin; in love with a kid named Jasper, a gangly, gap-toothed-kid I've known my whole life. Crawling floors as babies. Slobbering upon claw-foot chairs. Licking chicken poop before screaming parents could stop us. That's the wonderful thing about it, being together since birth. But that's also the terrible thing, for neither of us has been out of the county except for motocross races, and those places were all in East Tennessee, and folks here are pretty much all alike. Mostly.

Except, well... Jasper. He makes the world a better place. At least, he makes my world so. There are lots of things I need to tell about Jasper, but for now, just realize that we adore the same children's book, because it's much more than a kid's book. This wonderful thing is sort of an Ecclesiastes for kids, or a Proverbs for the puerile. We repeat little gems from this little book when inspired.

A French aviator named Antoine de Saint-Exupéry ran out of gas as he flew over North Africa, and the time he spent waiting in the desert inspired him to write *The Little Prince*.

While preparing for rescue, Saint-Exupéry met an alien visiting from a nearby heavenly body, Asteroid B-612. This space-alien Little Prince leaves home because he loved a certain flower, but they couldn't get along, so the Little Prince heads out and visits a King on *the planet of the king*, and this ruler turns out to be vain and narrow-minded. Imagine that.

The Little Prince next drops into Africa, meets the French aviator, and during their desert wanderings, they encounter a fox and a snake. The Little Prince learns a great deal about life from his desert time and his new teacher before returning to his asteroid home.

Their journey, subsequent hardships, and final departure leave a mark on the pilot.

Isn't Christianity based on the concept that life is a desert? The main characters of the *Old Testament* wandered 40 years. What they learn on the journey is the basis for the wisdom found in that book.

In the *New Testament*, Jesus ventures into the desert for 40 days to match wits with the Evil One.

There's a theme running through it. Cornelius and Sarge read *The Little Prince* to us when we were kids. They never preached to us. They just read that little book, in soft tones, a hundred times. More than *The Bible*, actually.

So Jasper and I have taken *The Little Prince*, made it ours, and share those desert moments of wisdom whenever they pop up and hit us in the face. You have to keep your eyes open and speak only when the desert moment uncloaks.

And here's the kicker. When I mentioned the book to you, Mr. Stephens, you said you loved it, as well. You had memorized whole sections. You and your wife Jewel repeat lines to each other constantly. Makes the hair on the back of my neck stand up.

In little Kituwah Falls, you make your own entertainment if you're not glued to electronics. But as soon as you're lost in the mountains to the east, the reception goes away.

Sure, we have TV and the internet and cell phones and iPads and iPods and iCrap of all kinds. And most people are holed up in the living room or basement, tapping buttons, basking in the glow of a high-definition flat screen. It's good training for a life stoned on opiates, I reckon.

But us, we don't fall into that trap. No. We have our desert, and we fill our desert moments. Together. Side by side.

Something I hope you, my babies, manage to also do in your time…

***

Kituwah Falls, once an ancient Cherokee trading post, is wired to the point that few venture outdoors for fun.

Neither Cornelius Whitlock—Jasper's dad—nor Sarge spent their childhoods indoors. Cornelius climbed every ridge he could see, kayaked every navigable stream, and drove his old Subaru with the kayak lashed on top to conquer others. Sarge ran trap lines as a teenager, hunted deer and turkey, fished for trout, rode dirt bikes twelve months out of the year, and became an Army Ranger before he was 23.

And because that's how these men grew up, it also affects our reality in a place where few, like I said, venture out, unless really necessary. For us, time indoors means sleeping, studying, cleaning, or cooking. We have computers for school, limited to homework time, or to look up words if the dictionary doesn't cut it. Cornelius turns us loose to research stuff now and then, if it's school-related.

Jasper and I grew up listening to 60's rhythm and blues, hearing things like *groovy, badass, bitchin', candy ass, dork, lay rubber, shag ass, raunchy, scarf, meanwhile, back at the ranch,* and a thousand other idioms that now naturally fall off our lips. When you grow up on Motown and The Who, well, Miley Cyrus and 50 Cent sound candy ass, and country songs about tractors sound stupid. My opinion. I do love Pharrell Williams, Shania Twain, Justin Timberlake, and tons of Americana bands; but the more old school, the better.

"Only the children know what they're looking for," said the Little Prince.

Mr. Reuben Stephens, my school counselor and college prep history teacher, isn't much like anyone around here, or maybe anywhere.

Though, I reckon, once you get to know them, folks are folks most anywhere in the world, in that they want to protect their families and do right by them.

giggle

I just read that back and it sounds awfully hillbilly, but that's my voice. I know English better than Kituwah, the Cherokee language. I can only recognize a few Kituwah words and phrases.

Sarge made a reader out of me, and I can tell in a heartbeat whether a writer is a reader or just a bullshit artist.

Well, kiddies, I already feel better after scratching this down on paper. This sweet black pencil is working its way across the page like a self-propelled word spreader, *Mirado Black Warrior HB2,* like lettering on an ammunition box. Wonderful lead, crappy eraser that fell out, leaving a gold-colored cylinder hole, sans pink piston, scratching through paper, making yellow holes when the pink is petered out.

But I'm still so pissed, still mad. All these words on thirsty white paper, and I can still see my fingers around Bo Wruck's throat, see his forehead in my rifle sights, feel the duct tape unspool to hold the car bomb in place under the driver's side floorboard of that creepy Escalade he borrows from his mom, who is fueled on pill money, prescription drugs.

You want to know how it all went down the drain? How everything turned for the worse? Yes, kids—let's face the elephant in the room, shall we? The bane of our little society, the highest grossing business in our lowly town, but under the table, off the books, safely out of the hands of the taxman.

17

"*If you get too cold I'll tax the heat, if you take a walk I'll tax your feet.*"

How many kids my age can quote George Harrison? Jasper, Amanda and I are Beatles fans and speak a secret Beatle language, you little piggies.

Life was so good before the invasion of the opioid-peddling mind-snatchers.

The Madisonville Advocate & Democrat

Ashley DeWitt Sizemore

Ashley DeWitt Sizemore of Kituwah Falls walked into the open arms of our Lord and Savior Friday March 18, 2016.

Born July 3, 2012 in Knoxville, Ashley loved making doll clothes and playing *family*. Her bright smile and loving nature will be missed by all.

Immediate survivors include parents Ted and Sylvia Sizer and seven siblings.

A memorial service will be held 6:30pm Sunday, March 21 at Hopewell Springs Baptist Church.

Miami

The Cubans: Ernesto Lemus, Javier Delgado, Jorge Fonseca.

The three lifelong friends sat on custom-made leather couches, watched the waves sparkle through giant bay windows in their work-condo on South Beach, and discussed business, like nearly every day in balmy Miami. All three light-skinned, loose-limbed, and oiled in expensive cocoa-hemp butter.

Ernesto—*the brains*—stood ramrod straight, inhaled no flake, sucked no weed, just sipped rum and juice at social functions. Nothing came between his consciousness and a business decision, entrepreneurial success the drug of his dreams, inflaming his waking moments. He read *Forbes, Robb Report, Money,* and *The Economist* religiously, purchased hookers three-days-a-week to fill the double-standard-Christian empty hole in his life, resulting in rumors he'd put out a hit on his own wife when she'd danced with an underling before his eyes at Las Tabernas De Wancho, a Miami hot spot. Then his second wife, 13 years his junior, had accepted a ring one week later.

He unconsciously pulled at his pants when they slipped below his narrow hips, a mannerism no one corrected, but all noticed. Ernesto drove every day to the cemetery and swept his parents' graves, pulling away dead flowers and leaving fresh roses.

Javier—*the wheel-greaser*—was the lean one with flawless skin and poor posture. Days leaning forward on the couch inhaling flake bent him at the shoulders. Neat and pleasant. Always smiling, but a business-wired brain flashing behind the dentist-fashioned caps. Extroverted, he loved to walk the city in lightweight Armani suits, meeting with the high echelon of the status quo in flashy restaurants, buying rounds of brown-rum mojitos here, suggesting the strawberry *pastelitos* there, keeping the wheels of the drug empire lubricated with endless cash outlays, his fun-loving nature capturing everyone's attention.

Jorge—*the enforcer*— had heavy brows over bulging black eyes, splotchy-brown skin, square-faced under thin hair, which stood like a hedge-row upon his wide head. He'd bullied weaker children throughout his youth, until Ernesto and Javier had greeted him with baseball bats in the alley behind the bungalows where Jorge was to meet a girl. Javier and Ernesto easily beat the older kid, focusing on shoulders and thighs, leaving his head unscathed. They admired his muscle, delighted in his lack of brains, and they enlisted Jorge to protect them from future physical threats.

Jorge enforced collections, following orders unquestioning. Consequently, success fell upon his knotty head like Cuban-tropical-rain.

Growing up wolf eyeing a kaleidoscope of skirts, and studying the myriad of pimps prancing up and down Calle Ocho, the three friends heard stories of heady-hot-soulful Havana days. The late-40's-early-50's, the casinos, the swarming prostitutes, estimates of 1,100 whores in a city of 100,000 souls. The hedonistic Americans streaming down from New York, Miami, Tampa, spending, whoring, drinking, gambling and, in a glorious-wide-open-era, their families growing rich as bribe-taking members of the Batista regime, their fathers having served in the military together during the Revolt of the Sergeants in the 30's, cozying up to the populist dictator, just as the American government and the New York mafia under Meyer Lansky wrapped their arms around Batista, despite democracy's loss and authoritarianism's gain.

The US government deported Lansky's friend and associate, Charles *Lucky* Luciano, to Sicily after Lansky consolidated the Jewish and Italian mafia into an intractable network of thugs, but Luciano traveled to Havana instead, setting the scene for the decades of cash flow into Batista bank accounts, and those of his cronies. The US finally pressured the dictator into deporting Luciano, but Meyer Lansky remained.

In the late 1940's, Batista agreed to allow Lansky's New York and Chicago gangsters into Havana, as long as he received gambling and racetrack kickbacks. Inexpensive marijuana and cocaine flowed through the city as freely as rum in those days. Meanwhile, native Cubans squatted in tin shacks across the land, survived on the scraps of the decimated sugar cane trade, and propped their barrios against the whitewashed walls of the casinos, while the Lemus, Fonseca, and Delgado families flourished, laying stacks of American greenbacks in Swiss bank accounts for a future they could not imagine.

When Fidel Castro and Ché Guevara organized the masses, who'd suffered through unemployment and lack of good drinking water for decades under the dictator, the Batista stronghold began to crumble. Seeing that firing squads or imprisonment loomed large—with nightmares of the French Revolution stealing their sleep—the three families crept out of Havana in the spring of 1959 on a private yacht, and immediately set up shop in Miami among wealthy ex-patriots. Some say a half-million Cubans jumped the island in 1959. The exodus dribbled through the early 1960's, with most emigrants pooling in the Capital of Latin America—Miami—or Fort Lauderdale.

Ernesto (1974), Jorge (1972), and Javier (1973) were born, educated, and raised among the elite of the Calle Ocho—Eighth Street, west of downtown—in an area locals called *Little Havana*.

Stories were all that remained of the Batista empire, stories the boys heard growing up in the 1980's, during the second wave of Cuban emigration—the 125,000 souls who didn't drown during the passage—nicknamed the Mariel Boat Lift, as Miami-dispatched-vessels swarmed the port city of Mariel. The latest wave in 1994 carried another 30,000 souls.

The 1959 assault was comprised mainly of light-skinned-upper-middle-class, or upper class Batista followers, but the later incursions consisted of mainly blacks and mulattoes. Cubans all.

And instead of warring with the lower-caste arrivals, Ernesto's father, Enrique—the business-genius-patriarch and closed-lipped leader of the three families—played the newcomers as pawns in his burgeoning cocaine-marijuana empire, making them the street-level dealers and subordinates, willingly filling Miami jails and Florida prisons for mental-comfort, knowing families would eat, even prosper.

This insulation, plus the monthly bags of money paid to the Miami status quo, kept the Lemus-Delgado-Fonseca families fat and secure for decades, until the first-wave old folks passed with festive funerals and warmly remembered legacies as the cocaine-marijuana trade morphed into the pill mill epidemic of today.

The significance of the green cash crop faded with legalization, for either medical and recreational use in several US states, and it nearly died when both Canada and Mexico relaxed laws and feinted toward legalization.

Cocaine still brought in significant returns, but the cost of living began to edge out their high-flung lifestyles, until the old but enduring *opiate of the masses*—religion—finally took second place to the new and instantly gratifying religion of the masses:

Opiates.

***

Ernesto, demonstrating managerial skills and a high IQ, at least when it came to running a drug business—though unable to bow to the compromises of marriage—

inherited the reins from Enrique in the early new millennium at the tender age of 27.

Those old stories of the Batista regime's mafia-fueled 1950's Havana, the boys' own experience at watching the drug trade skyrocket in 1980's Miami, and their life-long imbuement in Roman Catholicism, imprinted the clinical nature of their enterprise, plus the learned payoff of perseverance embedded straight into their street-smart skulls as they realized another wave would certainly follow the cocaine-marijuana epidemic, as surely as corruption rose throughout the ranks of the DEA, buoyed by bribes and threats—employing the narcos-worn-cliché *do you wish for gold or lead?*

Just as surely as heroin now followed on the footsteps of oxycodone, always a new wave, and deeper-more-satisfying-longer-lasting-skull-popping high, they became the iconoclastic entrepreneurial sharks, learning from the first wave of pill mill owners popping up throughout South Florida like gray mushrooms bursting toward sunlight on a hot April morning.

When the *tres amigos* realized that carloads of Georgians and Tennesseans flocked to gringo-owned South Florida Pain Management Clinics, Buicks, Cadillacs and Chevy station wagons full of over-weight, burger-sucking, diabetic-pill-seekers, risking highway death for hundreds of miles just to scarf down opiates, the boys quickly fired up their own enterprise farther north. They did Tampa, Jacksonville, then Albany, Macon, Atlanta, Chattanooga, and Knoxville—the most fertile ground yet discovered. High-unemployment, low-education, greed-for-cash, and a limitless hunger for prescription drugs previously unimagined by the Cubans.

One of their Tampa chiefs, Hillsborough County Pain Management Clinic's Odessa Blankenship, showed a remarkable ability to adapt new business practices whenever the legitimate authorities cropped up or state laws changed to try to thwart their enterprise. They leap-frogged her to Knoxville in 2010, and profits boomed.

Initially, the South Florida clinics were *owned* by local families that held long ties to the medical and banking communities, and they profited from their private stable of crooked physicians eager to over-prescribe opiates and rake in a percentage of profits.

In 2009, however, one story dominated the national news for two days, and became the reason for the Cubans' quick entrepreneurial move north.

Kris and Georgette Samuels, millionaire first cousins, co-owned a pill mill chain in South Florida specializing in Roxicodone, similar to oxycodone in chemical structure, and even more popular due to its lack of filler—aspirin or Ibuprofen often triggered stomach upset—and they raked in money from opiate-chomping Georgians and Tennesseans.

But six Tennesseans, after a three-hour-standing-wait outside the Samuels' PMC, scored 240 Roxicodone tablets each, stuffed themselves back into their worn-out-paint-chipped 2003 Dodge van, ate handfuls of roxies apiece, stopped at McDonald's for shakes and burgers, and stumbled back to their car at 2pm.

The roxies kicked in a few minutes later, just before the hollow-eyed driver snaked the vehicle midway through the horizontal train crossing warning poles, exposing the van's broadside to a commuter train flying 79 miles per hour toward Miami.

Splat.

Kris Samuels spoke candidly in her own defense, protesting to the judge: "Only an idiot would visit a pain management clinic, take too many drugs, then pull out in front of a train on the way home."

The Cubans, news-hounds and crime story-readers, adapted quickly when they realized the Opiate Express was leaving the station without them, and immediately financed clinics surrounding Tampa in drug-fertile, alcohol-fueled trailer parks spreading endlessly to central Florida hill country, quickly adopting Odessa's idea of employing sponsors who inflated profits exponentially.

Odessa met the challenge, recruited dozens like Leeza and Slowburn, grew the Tampa-area business, and when Florida cracked down on PMCs, the Cubans financed her move to opiate heaven: East Tennessee.

And when Odessa carried the Wruck Gang along for the ride, the Grim Reaper smiled at the easy tracks to follow.

The Madisonville Advocate & Democrat

Sidney James Hollyfield

Sidney James Hollyfield of Kituwah Falls passed away at home Saturday March 26, 2016. He was born April 3, 1981 in Knoxville.

Sidney worked as a Tennessee Department of Transportation truck mechanic and highway maintenance worker since graduating from Kituwah Falls High School in 1999. Sidney enjoyed being a pit-mechanic for several motocross teams in the area, and was known for his great sense of humor and practical jokes played on close friends.

He was 34.

Survivors include parents Andrew and Helen Hollyfield; wife Brenda Hollyfield; son Brendan Hollyfield; brother Mathew Hollyfield; and sister Jeanette Hollyfield.

A memorial service celebrating the life of Sidney Hollyfield will be held 6pm Friday, April 8 at Kituwah Falls Methodist Church.

Madisonville - Afghanistan – Kituwah Falls

James Tallent Walker—JT to folks at home—born squalling and slick with sweat and afterbirth on a rainy October 8th morning in the Madisonville hospital, never remembered the look, smell, or touch of his mother, who passed a week after his birth.

Died of doctors.

But JT retained her features—the wide forehead, the blazing black eyes, the quick temper fought back with prayer and lip-biting, the patience of planning and carrying out a goal to fruition woven into his fabric.

Don't start what you can't finish runs in the blood on both sides of the family.

***

The elementary school student immediately sized up the game of basketball: five like-minded players working together could defeat any team boasting a couple of hot shots. He'd also witnessed his mom and dad working in tandem. Successful farm life depended on teamwork.

When he made the high school varsity team as a sophomore, the two most-talented seniors, Randy Jeffers and Bobby Green, failed to accept the team-concept, bad-mouthed and abused younger players, and padded their stats while ignoring the win column.

Angered, JT met them after practice one late October afternoon, 1996. Broke both their noses, and knocked out Randy's buck teeth.

The demoralized seniors didn't heal quickly enough for the following Friday night game versus arch-rival Madisonville, and the KFHS Cherokees tromped the surprised Mustangs by eight points, united by 11 assists from point guard JT Walker, 12 rebounds by forward Cornelius Whitlock, 19 points from forward Luke Green, six steals by guard Jerrod Ferguson, and six blocked shots by center Jimmy Mills, as the sophomore-and-junior-led squad jelled into a cohesive five-man-unit. They clearly loved helping each other succeed, and now expressed it on the court sans the show-boaters, permanently benched upon their return. After a month of bench sitting, they left the team and badmouthed the coach behind his back. But the team's success merely exposed their thin skins.

Coach Smithpeters never said a word, except to the parents of the injured boys when they demanded punishment for JT's aggression.

"Two-on-one probably wasn't a fair fight," said a smiling Coach Smithpeters, "but your sons are bullies and deserved a whipping."

The coach did tell JT to channel his aggression in a positive way, and the boy heeded his advice, even throughout his military career.

The Cherokees went on to capture the regional title before finally suffering defeat to Knoxville Karnes, boasting a 1,500 student-population to Kituwah Falls' 250.

***

Pursuant to the authority vested in me as President by the Constitution and the laws of the United States of America, including section 112 of the Internal Revenue Code of 1986 (26 US C. 112), I designate, for purposes of that section, Afghanistan, including the airspace above, as an area in which Armed Forces of the United States are and have been engaged in combat.

For purposes of this order, I designate September 19, 2001, as the date of the commencement of combatant activities in such zone.

GEORGE W. BUSH
THE WHITE HOUSE
December 12, 2001

***

Sarge felt mixed over this executive order. He realized the need to strike back at the terrorists who'd made 9/11 a day of infamy, surpassing even the Japanese sneak attack on Pearl Harbor.

But the terrorists were nearly all Saudi nationals. Sure, many of them had trained in Afghanistan, but so did bin Laden, who'd trained under American advisors who'd helped the Afghanis defeat the Russian Army in the Soviet-Afghan War, with our Stinger Missiles transported on the backs of Tennessee mules.

Sarge knew JT understood the history of Afghanistan: after countless invasions, no one stayed. Ever.

The US helped defeat the Russians after they invaded Afghanistan in 1979, but as soon as they were gone ten years later, running back to vodka and shashlik, with their tails between their legs, we packed up and flew home, as well.

Had we stayed to rebuild schools, supply electricity to villages, and prevent the government from falling down the corruption hole, bin Laden, al-Qaida, and the Taliban would never have risen to power.

Our indifference following the Soviet-Afghan War created 9/11.

Sarge followed history, and doubted Americans would concentrate on Afghanistan long enough to win, which proved to be prescient. No one else hung around long enough to win.

Reading history taught him that the public often felt victory would arrive in the first few weeks—a physiological trap luring the nation into years-long campaigns, draining blood and treasure.

Ill-conceived invasions led to US troops trickling back in flag-draped coffins.

Sarge had lived through all that before, witnessing early victories in Vietnam—victories all through the war, actually. The Tet Offensive was a huge military victory for US combat troops, but it played differently on TV and in the press, and all the wins eventually led to defeat and loss of heart and face.

Won the battles. Lost the war.

Pyrrhus defeating the Romans at Heraclea. *Ad infinitum.*

Invaders never tarried in Vietnam, Iraq, or Afghanistan.

During the First Gulf War, George H. W. Bush, an actual combat veteran, became skeptical of US and UK citizens sitting in bars thumping chests, cheering radar-controlled missiles, and exhibiting the bravery-of-being-out-of-range, and knew instinctively that moving on Baghdad would incur uncountable losses—as his Texas National Guard AWOL all-hat-no-cattle son discovered, to his perpetual chagrin—and so the First Gulf War wrapped up in 100 days under the commonsense leadership of a WWII veteran. George H. W. recognized the error of Vietnam, but failed to pass on the knowledge that conquering a country meant perpetual occupation. Or failure.

***

JT graduated from high school in the middle of his class, and could not conjure up a good reason to go to college. With tobacco losing its national cool, JT's ambivalence toward bovines, and with three generations of ranger riflemen behind him, he signed up for the US Army, completed his basic training at Fort Benning, Georgia, and then volunteered to become a member of the 75th Ranger Regiment.

Physical and mental requirements posed no problem, but one thing bothered him: which specialty should he pursue?

The 70-plus choices overwhelmed him. None appeared related to motorcycling, although he thought they'd be a wonderful operations tool, and to his chagrin, he found out late in his enlistment that special-operation-motorcycles often met the task of rough terrain surveillance.

Loving every minute of basic training, JT looked over the list of Occupational Specialist positions and picked the only thing that made sense to him: 11B. Infantry. Rifleman.

Zeke. Pap. Sarge. Now it was JT's turn.

Sarge made his feelings clear before JT signed up. "It's tough raising a kid as a single parent," said Sarge. "But going off to war will put it back on me. And we've had enough riflemen in the family. We sacrificed our share."

"Well," smiled JT, "you certainly did a great job raising me." A tear dripped down his cheeks. "I'll be back soon enough. And then, I'll never leave her again, at least until she's married or off on her own."

Sarge shed saltwater, as well, knowing how prescient those words might be.

Losing Leeza stung his heart, but it nearly imploded when he left Samantha home with Sarge. The one problem he couldn't shirk—deployment—as an active member of the military when his unit flew to Afghanistan three weeks after he graduated ranger school paratrooper training, right after he'd turned 22.

Congress never declared war, but terrorist training camps begged for eradication, so there he was, separated by an ocean, and half-a-world from his daughter.

Leeza's whereabouts were unknown, but he guessed that Digger offered business training, and she spent her days soaking it up with entrepreneurial zeal.

Two weeks from discharge in 2003, JT had volunteered to join a rescue team rushing out to recover a ground-force-assault-infiltration-team taking heavy fire from the Taliban.

"Stay back here, JT," his commanding officer pleaded. "Two weeks and you're back in Tennessee with your daughter."

JT smiled and said, "You'd volunteer if I were out there."

The CO hung his head, then watched misty-eyed as JT and his squad of volunteers helicoptered out into harm's way.

Always the team player. Always watching his partners' six. Always the servant-leader all loved, admired, followed.

***

Taught to hunt, to fish, and to labor by Sarge, JT loved farming, and planned to return to the land after his Gulf War deployment. And he did, but as fertilizer, not living flesh, lying stone-cold-prone in a rosewood box draped in the red-white-and-blue the Walkers planted in the family plot near the woods.

They buried him in 2003 alongside Zeke, Sally, Pap, and Esther, facing east, the Promised Land, and the Tellico River.

Five-year-old Samantha—all brown-skinny-arms-and-legs—stood next to Sarge, blinking, captivated by the townspeople covering their farm, the choking Presbyterian minister shaking in his black vestments, the emotional wave of the four-part-harmony singers wondering in melodious words about an unbroken circle. Sam erupted spontaneously when Sarge wept, not knowing why, silently provoked by adults wailing in unison, moved to shudders by adult tears flowing onto the lapels of Sarge's green service uniform.

Four ranger riflemen, third-in-line still standing.

Sarge. Alone with a little girl. Alone with a child in his arms a second time.

He'd learn to deal with it, to complete the task of raising her, and teach her the ways of the forest, prepare her for life. In those days following JT's death, Sarge sat in the shop with Samantha on his lap and looked at the frame-skeletons leaning against the walls.

Motorcycling had been JT's forte; he could ride or wrench with equal aplomb. The first year he was allowed to ride, the energy-filled–ten-year-old traipsed back into the house only to eat and sleep. Otherwise, if he wasn't in the shop wrenching, or out in the woods riding, he was in school and looking out the window, dreaming of wrenching and riding.

Sarge peered into the shaded north wall of his shop and counted eleven skeleton bikes lined up like refugees in a soup line, mostly just frames at this point, motorcycles he, JT, and Cornelius rode to death and left for parts, the mechanical-loves of JT's life age ten-to-whenever he met Leeza. Seventeen?

She'd used her ability to glide with the bike, sitting above the rear wheel, behind the decision-maker, keeping perfect balance, seemingly a part of the machine, a talent appreciated by those responsible for safely twisting through the sweepers two up at high speed.

Sarge surveyed the wreckage: a '69 Yamaha 250cc DT-1B; a '67 Triumph Tiger Cub with a gigantic-tree-climber rear sprocket; a '68 CT-90 Honda Trail; a black '67 Honda 305cc Dream; a '68 Ducati 250 Scrambler; a '69 Ducati Sebring 350; a '72 Suzuki TM-250; and clear in the back, next to a rusted barrel of long-gone motor oil, JT's very first motorbike, a barely-recognizable '69 four-speed Sears 106 Super Sport, made in Italy by Gilera, nine horsepower and capable of 58 miles-per-hour—downhill, with the wind at your back.

All of these bikes—old and worn out when bought. Usually at auction. Sarge smiled at that golden window of years, the decade he, JT, and Cornelius wrenched and rode together, pulling more miles out of gasping machines, endless laps to Morristown, snaking through the old buildings, ankle deep in water, green-brown-mold inching down the walls, ferreting out parts and hauling them back by the bushel.

Now only two bikes remained intact.

Sarge balanced Sam on his knee and walked over to Ole Blue, the CB-350G he'd straddled cross-country back into The World post-Vietnam.

Ole Blue, the patriarch of the part-filled yard-behind-the-barn.

"This will be yours," Sarge whispered to Sam. "Along with the farm and the legacy."

Afghanistan

Dear Samantha,

Hey, sweetheart. Daddy always seems to be in the field when the satellite phone is up, so I'll just drop a note into the box and let those big transports wing it to you.

Nothing hurts more than being away from you and Sarge, but I'll be home soon, for good.

In the meantime, know that you are loved and that we'll be exploring the Cherokee Forest together, fishing, kayaking, learning to handle a rifle, and getting to ride Ole Blue before you know it.

Perhaps those aren't girl things, but Sarge and I can only share what we know. Your grandmother would have known what to do, and Lois can help round off your edges, but I'm afraid the guy things are what we have to offer. And our hearts.

Luckily, your grandfather confirms my suspicions that you're a natural tomboy, so perhaps we're not messing you up too much by keeping you in the woods searching for morels, or in the river with a paddle in your hand and a smile on your face.

Only three weeks and I'll transfer home to The World! Hang on, baby!

Love you with all my heart and soul,
Dad

Bo Wruck's Journal

My first name is Garrett, but everyone calls me Bo. Short for Bocephus. You'd have to be familiar with old country music to understand.

And if you already get the connection, you know that one Bocephus sticker next to a *Semper Fi* decal on the back of your vehicle means you can park it anywhere in Appalachia without fear of it being stolen or damaged. Those two bumper stickers are as good as an electric force field here in the South.

Anyway, I ain't much at writing because I ain't much at reading, never liked it, makes my head hurt with all those images flocking into my brain all on their own rackety wings, willy-nilly, like a colony of bats set loose from Satan's lair straight into my head.

But I'm okay at talking, and Mr. Stephens says it's okay to write like I'm talking. He even said some serious writers take a lifetime to write like they're talking, but so far, it doesn't seem like any big deal. I'm just trying to keep my arm moving, and these words flowing, and meet the conditions of my probation officer and get on with my life, and make some big money to finance my racing dreams, and someday fly to motocross events, like the top five riders in the country, and hit those jumps fresh, get a little practice on the unknown tracks for a day or two, instead of driving across the country, eating greasy food and swallowing speed and sleeping little and being in no shape, hardly ever, to compete with those big dogs.

Life's unfair like that. Unless you trample a few little dogs and punch your own ticket.

But I'm getting ahead of myself. Really, I'm just a high school senior, racing the local Tennessee tracks, hoping to win this year's Motocross School Boy Division Championship. I am the number one rider on this small county circuit, after all.

With only one local rider who can come close to challenging me, Sam Walker. She's pretty good, too. I think I'm better because I ain't afraid of pushing the limit, hanging it out there. She desires a life in medicine, college at UT. She don't want the pro-motocross circuit like me.

Sam Walker has to keep a journal, too, but that's for anger management. Seems she can't get over that fall she took at the end of last season's championship Moto. Hurt her bad, the pain and all. Shoulder in a sling all Christmas break. She squirmed around and cried for a couple of weeks, but I took care of it.

That's my job.

The Madisonville Advocate & Democrat

Glenda-Jane Jackson

Glenda-Jane Jackson of Mount Vernon passed at home March 30, 2016. Born November 11, 1975 in Maryville, Jackson worked as a licensed practical nurse in several area retirement homes after graduating Chattanooga State Community College in 1995.

She enjoyed quilting, volunteer projects through Mount Vernon Baptist Church, and spending time with friends and family. She loved socializing with friends and medical acquaintances.

She was 40.

Survivors include parents Jonathan and Marilyn Jackson, and sister Betty-Ann Jackson. A memorial will be held 6:30pm Saturday, April 9 at Mount Vernon Baptist Church.

Seattle to Kituwah Falls

Sarge mounted the 350G Honda, fired it up, and rode down the California coast to San Diego, across to Phoenix, out to Albuquerque, up to Farmington, New Mexico, the joyous ride across the mountainous pass into Colorado, Durango, Silverton, Ouray, then a long jaunt around to Montrose, over to Telluride, the first city in America to enjoy alternating current—Nikola Tesla had picked a box canyon out in the middle of nowhere to try out his idea, in case it failed, so no one would ever know—over to Grand Junction, up to Buena Vista, Leadville, Aspen, Independence Pass, Winter Park, across Estes Park to Boulder. He fell in love with a younger set of Colorado mountains, just getting past their teenage years, only 170 million years old, unlike the geriatric Appalachians, bent and vegetation-covered, 450 million years old. Then it was out into the prairie sprawling east of Denver, and he gasped at its immensity, a vast table as wide as the sea, with the same optical bent and curve as the ocean, and he daydreamed of using a sextant to mark his spot in the universe, should he lose the map.

The calming effect of viewing the country from a motorcycle helped him decide it was worth the effort, his service in Vietnam, regardless of the way some people treated him and his service buddies when they returned to The World. The spitting. The accusing screams: baby killer!

The price of democracy.

Sarge knew that some wars were ill conceived at the start; they tore holes in the nation's fabric. His war ripped a gaping fissure that failed to properly heal.

Sarge didn't see the point in interfering with sovereign nations, bitch-slapping entire races of people we didn't understand. As a heterogeneous mix of blue bloods, blue-collar workers, immigrants, Native Americans, Canadians,

Mexicans, and foreigners of every color, religion, creed, and caste—we didn't even understand ourselves, much less people living on the other side of the planet.

The Vietnam experience taught him that the lower case *world* of the Orient was so foreign, so odd, and so otherworldly, that soldiers thought of their own World with a capital letter.

Many soldiers wrote letters back to The World, and he wrote often. His mother gave the letters back to him after his dad passed. And after his mother died, he never re-read them, or ever considered perusing them again, knowing it would open old wounds, as he felt no man had enjoyed better parents, more loving, generous, but steely-eyed, progenitors.

They'd worked him sweaty with farm labor, kept an eye on his grades, held high expectations after high school, and gifted him with confidence by teaching perseverance. He understood the value of failure, the tempering of the soul through service, and the requirement to remain productive in the brutal face of one's naturally short existence.

After witnessing so many dysfunctional families in law-enforcement and EMT careers—a Forest Service ranger has to protect the park, which means dealing with the low-life—he knew he'd been extremely lucky being drafted by his parents.

"Don't start anything you can't finish," falls out of Sarge's lips as his personal identification phrase, his philosophy-of-life, his future epitaph.

***

Pap had served in the European Theater, carrying a Springfield M1 carbine, surviving three major battles.

Celebrating with his brothers-in-arms on 8 May 1945, aka VE Day, Pap believed he'd travel home soon to his sweetheart Esther and his parents Zeke and Sally.

But after the victory party ended and the hangovers passed, his company learned that in two days, they'd be transported through the Panama Canal on a troop transport headed to Japan.

To be part of a million-man assault upon a country still teeming with subjects loyal to an Emperor hijacked by the state, a race of people who routinely wrapped themselves in hand-grenade belts and leaped out of trees onto unsuspecting patrols.

Pap told Sarge he often felt sad picking off Germans. He knew they'd been tricked by the political chicanery of Hitler, that the Great Depression caused the Germans to temporarily lose their minds, and that, given the chance, like Americans and Brits, would share a meal and talk of the family back home rather than blast each other into eternity. He'd talked to several prisoners, through interpreters, and one who spoke a little broken English. The Weimar Republic servicemen tended to exhibit shame for their link to Hitler, and they especially hated the SS. Pap shot Weimar soldiers all day long when possible, but he also recognized they weren't much different from himself, defending their country, despite the insane policies of its leadership.

But the Japanese?

Pap and his fellow European Theater veterans all realized the end of their voyage meant almost certain death, and they held their voices on the way over the Atlantic, across the Canal, and into the Pacific heading west, the bunks and passageways and mess halls a deadly quiet as they contemplated their fate.

So when a patrol-torpedo-boat materialized out of the mist, floated into their path, hailed the captain on the radio, and forced the transport to slow down to idle, they threw a skeptical eye on the proceedings.

When the little boat's captain boarded and announced, "The War is over!" and that we'd dropped some kind of new bomb on the Japs, no one swallowed it.

Believing it was a joke or elaborate scam to get a rise out of them, some sort of fraternity joke played between naval officers, they nearly ripped the arms and legs off the poor fellow before the news was confirmed by a radio broadcast from a passing surveillance plane. They suddenly shouted in unison, eyes wet with relief, some going to their knees in thanksgiving, all realizing they'd been spared twice in as many months. And then suddenly, as if on cue, the engines fired back up, the transport slowly wheeled in the foam, the ship groaned in a wide arc to face America, heading east to The World they'd nearly perished to preserve. And they knew it was true: They would live.

Pap returned to Kituwah Falls, rejoined his blood family, then his church family, married his high school sweetheart, Esther Mills, from a good Presbyterian family, farmed his small piece, worked in mills during the winter months, and doubled the farm to 120 acres over the next 15 years.

When the losses mounted, after his wife joined Zeke and Sally in The Promised Land, reunited with her parents Jedidiah and Elizabeth Mills; after the long diminuendo to death, breast cancer's virtuoso performance; after Vane left for Vietnam and Pap was left to his thoughts in the depths of his dotage, he realized that experience, death, and the ongoing loss of mental and physical strength tempered his optimism. He never blamed God for his woes, but thanked Him for the many blessings he'd enjoyed throughout a long and fruitful life. Pap told Sarge that thankfulness and gratitude were essential elements of a clear conscience, markers of positive mental health.

***

Sarge absorbed his father's philosophy through osmosis, spending many days alone with Pap, working side-by-side with the veteran rifleman, hoeing tobacco, running trap lines, hunting, fishing, skinning, cooking, loving every minute of a life lived outdoors, and the quiet generosity and endless love of a father whose ego flowered in deeds, not words.

On his second tour, he and his troop of eight rangers found themselves in deep jungle, sleuthing the Ho Chi Min Trail, surveilling troop strength, supply availability, and depth of munitions. They reached the Cambodian border four days after parachuting into a safe zone, and on the third day of the stakeout, before any of the teenaged and wiry-looking NVA slipped down the path, an ear-splitting scream pierced the air.

Sarge and his men swung their heads around, like a school of fish. Their mouths fell open at the sight of Corporal Sorrell dragged by the thigh into the shaded green by a fire-eyed Bengal tiger, Sorrell's screams raising hackles up and down the line of young men.

Sarge hesitated for a long moment, then rushed on, tracking the animal for the remainder of the afternoon, but neither beast nor Sorrell were eyeballed again.

The dream of that dark adventure stole his sleep, and every so often, the darkest of nightmares sat him straight up in bed, shivering, sweat popping from his brow, and a clear vision summoning the horror of the giant cat, squatting on a trail, feeding the enemy men and materiel, squatting and growling and pushing and forcing a United States ranger turd out onto a land we never should have invaded in the first place.

That was enough proof of the folly of invasion, the symbol of bad policy, the acknowledgement of a war fought for Capitalism, for Goodyear and Firestone, Boeing and General Electric, Dow Chemicals and Northrup Grumman, Martin-Marietta, Lockheed, Bell, and Mattel, who marketed plastic replicas of the M16 to children. And for a soldier in the field, it was comforting to look down the stock of your M16 and see the toy manufacturer's name imprinted on a weapon that froze up in the rain and mud.

"All you have to do is keep it clean," said boot camp Drill Instructor Winston Thorogood, who they assumed knew what he was talking about, as he was there to preserve their lives through training.

But after the jungle rain fell and the dirt worked deep into their skin and jungle rot sprouted on their toes, they slept little and cleaned much as they wiped and re-wiped and dried their weapons, while the NVA slept and dreamed of a free sovereign nation defended by the ubiquitous Soviet AK-47, full of mud and water and spit and blood and firing, forget the damn cleaning and wiping. Sleep and dream and rise and fire and kill; yes, the NVA may lose a half-million, some estimated as much as eight million. It didn't matter how high the final body count rose, because at some proud point, the enemy, once the Chinese, then the French, and lately the Americans, would fold its tent, hang its head, and fly home with its proverbial tail between its bowed cowboy legs.

The Vietnamese watched them come and go. Eight times. No one ever stayed.

And did *we* learn?

Iraq. Afghanistan. And on it goes.

Sarge refused to mock folks whose families had been systematically torn apart over the 200-plus years of slavery leading up to the Civil War. Drawing great parents and then putting down folks not so fortunate was the dominion of small minds.

***

Sarge's great-grandmother was a half-blood Cherokee nicknamed Sally by her husband, Ezekiel Walker, a tall, wiry Scot who'd hiked into Western North Carolina two years after landing in America, three years after returning to his hometown of Neilston, Scotland, ten miles southwest of Glasgow, in the bloody wake of WWI, and finding the village distraught and young-manless. Britain did not send coffins back to soldiers' home villages for burial. KIA's were planted where they fell, usually in France or Belgium. Had the townspeople eyeballed the effect of graveyards blossoming in all directions with the ripe remains of 888,246 of their young sons, the War would have ended too quickly for the British government to declare victory.

One-hundred sixty-four of Neilston's finest never returned from the killing fields, and Zeke had witnessed 16 of his brothers-in-arms choke to death one September afternoon in 1915 at The Battle of Loos—he was 18 at the time. Phosphine, a colorless, flammable gas, blew back into their faces when the wind suddenly reversed direction.

This was the first time the Brits had used gas on the battlefield. After the wind shifted, soldiers' goggles rapidly dimmed over, and insufficient amounts of filtered air were allowed into their lungs.

Sixteen men lost patience, pulled off their masks, and perished. Zeke kept his mask in place, fought off the urge to panic, buried his head between his knees, using prayer to pull his heart rate down until the vaporous cloud fell to the ground in the absence of wind.

When The War to End All Wars eventually decrescendoed to a halt, returning soldiers unwittingly carried the Spanish Flu pandemic back to their homes all around the planet, killing 500 million civilians. The village morphed into a dormitory city, what we call a bedroom community, a place outside an industrialized area where laborers dwelled between long shifts.

Young Zeke wanted none of that.

He'd been spared, for some odd reason, inflaming his guilt, and he felt it was his duty to make something of his life.

So after a year of wandering the countryside, thinking things through, he hugged his parents goodbye and boarded a steamer in Glasgow bound for St. Johns, Nova Scotia, in 1919.

The bitter climate and lack of jobs drove him south, and he wandered down the north Appalachians into Front Royal, Maryland, down the Shenandoah Valley into Western North Carolina, and down the gravel roads and creek fords of East Tennessee, where he finally settled in Kituwah Falls. The natural beauty of the mountain forests, falling like the pure Tellico River into the Tellico Plains of northwestern Monroe County, captured his heart.

"The best of both worlds," he mused to himself.

Endless mountains to the east, bursting with fish, game, and timber; plus the river-bottom richness of a tillable plain, side-by-side, begging for someone to take this Cherokee paradise—minus most of the Cherokee—and shape it into a wilderness playground.

The Babcock Lumber Company immediately hired Zeke at two dollars a day, which was actually better than the national average for wages in 1921.

Babcock Lumber, the first and last true economic engine of Kituwah Falls, clear-cut the forest from the east edge of town all the way to the ridgeline—125,000 acres— from 1905 until 1933, when it sold most of its land to the US Forest Service. The Cherokee National Forest and the Great Smoky National Park later absorbed nearly all of this parcel.

The old logging road built to harvest roughly 1,000 train car loads a day, is now State Route 165, the fabled Cherohala Skyway, 43 miles of motorcycle heaven running all the way to Robbinsville, North Carolina, after morphing into North Carolina State Route 143 at the border.

The runoff from the naked mountainsides choked the Tellico River for years, causing havoc on the Walker farm, but Zeke persevered. After three years of lumbering and living a lonely bachelor existence in a lumber camp tent, he was able to purchase 60 acres of tillable soil north of town, in the heart of the Tellico Plain.

In the spring of '22, he planted his first tobacco crop and a patch of corn to lure the deer and fatten the two pigs that he'd won in a poker match one Saturday night at the Tellico Tavern. With little time to build a cabin between the growing season, suckering, and the harvest, he hired back on with Babcock and spent the winter in a dormitory tent, cut the timber for his own cabin walls from the few trees left standing on the property, and finally roofed it in July after suckering the tobacco.

That fall, he hung the cash crop in the vacant barn of a neighbor.

Following the pioneer practices of the Scot-Irish before him, he relied heavily on his friends and neighbors, as it took a group effort to survive in the rocky-field dirt of the Southeast, and they often invited him to worship.

And although the killing fields of France caused him to question the benevolence of his Creator, social life revolved around the church, and Zeke was quickly drawn into the arms of Kituwah Presbyterian, which immediately became his family and system of support.

A deal sealed twice.

First, there were the Tellico Boys of The Fighting M Company, 117th Infantry Regiment, 30th Division, who also fought in France and Belgium, and returned to labor in the logging camps and to raise families on the plains of Monroe County. James Scott, Harold Moore, and Conrad Daniels knew what he'd seen, and all became as close as brothers in a few months. They'd also left 400 of their regional friends of the 117th buried beneath the long white headstones of Ypres.

One rainy spring Sunday in 1925, a family from across the mountain in Cheoah Township, Graham County, North Carolina, sat in the west second row pews of Kituwah Presbyterian Church, founded just two years earlier by the Reverend Davis Bartleby. After the service, Zeke introduced himself to the lanky, dark-skinned, curly-haired Josiah Campbell, his pretty wife Bly, and 17 year-old daughter Salali.

Campbell crossed the mountain for the opportunity to work for Babcock, who wanted able-bodied men to show up, work all day, and cause no trouble after hours. The lumber company managers hired without regard to race, religion, or skin color in those days, when labor requirements dwarfed prejudice.

Clearing the trees and raking in the cash were Babcock's prime concerns.

And it didn't bother Zeke that the Campbells appeared to carry Melungeons' blood, putting faces to the dusky-skinned, curly-haired tribe of unknown origin.

The Caucasian population of Monroe County often discouraged their own from marrying people of this ilk, but Reverend Bartleby welcomed anybody who loved the Lord, and treated folks as *Matthew 25:40* commanded. The *New Testament* meant there was a new covenant with the One, and Bartleby honored it, despite the prejudice of the local population, and the Presbyterian doctrine of the elect, that he just did not buy into after years of prayer and study about church doctrine, and after years of examining the human heart. He'd learned the value of looking at people one-at-a-time, and realized the folly in scapegoating entire races on the habits of a few.

Kituwah Falls Presbyterian's congregation grew steadily throughout the 20's and 30's, with this open-minded, people-loving pastor leading the way.

Melungeons tended to stick to their own, or to marry blacks or Indians, a habit born from the pervasive discrimination experienced during the pioneer days, and true to form, Bly was full Cherokee, a remnant of the Eastern Band that fled to the mountains when Andy Jackson arrived to round up the Cherokee for their walk to Oklahoma.

Zeke didn't view any man willing to work as *the least of these*, and the fact remained: Salali, who was taller than Zeke, with raven black hair and a quick smile, was a clean-skinned beauty he could not avoid seeing in his mind's eye, neither awake nor asleep.

Josiah Campbell's natural fit into the Babcock labor pool meant his family safely took root in Monroe County. He and Zeke worked side-by-side most days, as Zeke slowly won Josiah's confidence.

The following spring, on Sally's 18th birthday, following a two-month courtship, they became Mr. and Mrs. Ezekiel Walker.

Sally proved to be a formidable partner, who understood the concept of teamwork so well that the Walker farm flourished. Their son, George, arrived a year-and-a-month later after Sally tossed down the tobacco hoe in the noonday sun, squatted in the shade of a sycamore, and pushed out his slick, squalling soul onto the dark loam of the Tellico River flood plain.

Monroe County Hospital

Martha battled a cough and a wheezy chest since catching cold in September of 1980, and on the 15th, feeling sick but walking under her own power a week after delivering JT, trudged through the doors of her doom.

With their family doctor Jon Green out of town for the week, Martha visited the Sweetwater Clinic, and was prescribed penicillin. But she broke out in a whole-body rash for the first time in her life—the mold-driven cure never having caused a problem before—so they drove the 30 minutes to Maryville, checking into County Hospital, which worried Sarge, as he'd heard a myriad of bad-ending stories connected to the place. But it was the hospital assigned to Dr. Green, their old friend at Kituwah Presbyterian, and family physician since they'd married.

Martha said she felt swimmy-headed and woozy in the stomach, but walked in under her own power. She still had an appetite and plenty of strength.

After filling out all the papers and being wheeled into a room, they noticed puddles of water on the floor. The thermostat in the corner read 97 degrees.

Sarge raised hell, but as they were overwhelmed with patients, the staff ignored his complaints. Martha breathed that hot, humid air and gasped for breath, and didn't see a doctor until the next morning, and she was unable to get a suitable room until late that afternoon.

A young hospital intern diagnosed her with viral pneumonia and prescribed penicillin, which Sarge argued would not affect a virus, but he kept his mouth shut after the doctor said he'd prescribed antibiotics in case his diagnosis was incorrect.

Three more doctors paraded through the room the morning after, each giving a different diagnosis: sarcoidosis, pleurisy, and lung cancer. Lung cancer! Martha never let a cigarette pass her lips, and she lived most of her life outdoors. Skin cancer, okay. Lung cancer?

Enraged, Sarge called Ed Trent, who had an old friend in the insurance business.

"These hospital docs can charge a hundred dollars a pop just for a visit and a diagnosis," Ed informed. "They really don't care if they scare the holy bejesus out of you. They need to make a boat payment, I reckon."

Knowing Martha lay writhing with pneumonia, and knowing the symptoms well from Vietnam, Sarge called Dr. Green, still with family in Johnson City, and begged him for help.

"I'll drive right down as soon as possible," said Dr. Green.

*　*　*

Martha said she felt stable, so Sarge took JT back to Kituwah Falls to let Ed look after him.

The day nurse, a 62 year-old veteran caregiver with a sweet bedside manner, told Martha that she was going off shift, and that the hospital doctor had prescribed a new antibiotic, Amoxicillin, because the penicillin was not working.

Martha nodded.

"If anything goes wrong, just push the call button," the nurse said.

The evening nurse, in her late twenties, hair dyed dark purple, sporting a hangover, with tattoos on both arms, her neck, and right foot, immediately began her shift by stepping outside to smoke a cigarette at the same moment the new antibiotic hit Martha's bloodstream.

Martha's eyes glassed over, a flush washed over her arms and face. She tried to push the call button, but her hand wouldn't operate. She tried to scream, but her throat locked.

Forty minutes later, the tattooed, tobacco-ed nurse reappeared, but Martha's temperature had already spiked to 106 degrees.

When Sarge arrived, Martha lay motionless, up to her neck in ice-cubes, a plastic sheet beneath her, while three fans blew wide open across her sweaty body.

She flat-lined 30 minutes later from anaphylactic shock.

Security ganged up and prevented Sarge from strangling the nurse, and Dr. Green arrived just in time to pronounce Martha dead, and wheeled her to the basement morgue.

The Madisonville Advocate & Democrat

Dylan Lyle Dykes

Dylan Lyle Dykes of Hopewell Springs passed at home April 23, 2016. Born February 25, 1994 in Maryville, Dylan was a carpenter and general handyman since graduating Madisonville High School in 2011. He completed courses at Pellissippi State Community College for a construction business principles certificate.

Dylan officiated motocross races as flagman at local tracks. Other hobbies included fishing and kayaking, deer and turkey hunting with friends.

He was 22.

Survivors include parents Sam and Dorothy Dykes, sister Jolene Dykes, and girlfriend Linda Samuels.

A memorial service will be held 6:30pm Monday, May 2 at Hopewell Springs Baptist Church.

Kituwah Falls High School Football Field

Modern turkey shoots, a far cry from the Sergeant York-movie days of plugging an actual tom turkey that's intermittently poking its head out from behind a horizontal log, involves no skill.

Each participant wields a 12-gauge shotgun with a universal barrel-end examined before the shoot, blasts a paper target from 56 to 90 feet away, peppering a drawn circle with standard buckshot. The circle holds a pinprick in its center.

Shooters pay an entry fee, usually $20, for the chance to pepper four targets, plus $3 a shell, handed out before each round by an un-connected third party.

No one is allowed to bring their own shells to a match, eliminating tampering, like covering the shot with animal fat, which would mass the pellets.

Judges count the number of pellets penetrating the circle of each target, adding the number of buckshot holes, plus the pinprick touches and pinpricks obliterated.

The shooter with the highest number of scores compiled from the four target circles takes home the meat, usually in the form of bologna, bacon, steak, ham, turkey, chops, perhaps a side-of-beef, or a whole hog, if large participation warrants the prize.

Winning a modern turkey shoot is a matter of chance, like pulling the lever on a slot machine or spinning a roulette wheel, as nearly anyone able to hold a gun can shotgun a still paper target at 56 to 90 feet.

Kituwah Falls High School, however, home to a large population of deer, turkey, squirrel, and rabbit hunters, holds an annual Old Settlers' Turkey Shoot the last Saturday each March. Participants and audience members dress up in frontier costumes, emulating the long rifle days of the Overmountain Men of the Revolutionary War period, who trekked across the Southern Appalachians to South

Carolina and confronted British Major Patrick Ferguson's troops at Kings Mountain.

Instead of turkeys, shooters aim at thick cardboard cutouts, hand-painted like tom turkeys and staked at the end of the football field, which terminates before a bullet-soaking dirt bank 20 yards beyond its perimeter. And they forego the shotgun blast for the pin prick of a .22 round.

Firing five .22-caliber long rifle bullets from a personal weapon of choice, using straight sights—no scopes—the winner scores the highest number of heart-or-head shots, cardboard turkey hearts and heads painted bright red for sighting. Participants stand at the opposite goal line and attempt to penetrate targets at 100 yards.

Sam arrived with Jasper, Sarge, Cornelius, Ed, and Lois Bailey a half-hour before the event, all but Lois dressed as male frontiersman, in buckskin coats and breeches, sporting wide black tricorn hats lovingly designed and sewn by Mrs. Bailey, who wore a free-flowing green denim dress covered with a loose green-and-white checked gingham shirt *à la* Annie Oakley. They mingled with the other hundred-plus participants, enjoying each other's costumes and attempting the British-influenced speech of the Revolutionary War period, giggling at each other's tongue troubles.

Each shooter paid $20 to enter the contest, the money going to the local food pantry for indigent families throughout the county, but the absence of prize money for the winner did not lessen the competitive nature of the event, the winner gaining bragging rights for the whole year.

Down to the last bullet, only three remained at the firing line.

Sarge, Sunny Wruck—Bo's twin brother, dressed in dirty jeans and a Bad Religion T-shirt—plus Sam.

Sarge held his gun loosely in front of him, aimed without sighting down the barrel, and placed a round over

56

his turkey-target into the bank, kicking up a small cloud of dirt.

"What are you doing?" asked Sunny.

"Letting you two youngsters have a go," said Sarge. "I've won this thing every year for the last 15 years."

"Stupid old man," said Sunny under his breath before quickly sighting, then squeezing the trigger on his CZ-USA Varmint bolt action target rifle, placing a round barely off the right edge of his target's turkey heart, a near-miss confirmed by the spotter glassing the contest with unwavering tripod-mounted-binoculars before Sunny protested, then looked for himself, cursing.

Sam slowly shouldered her Henry AR-7 Survival Rifle, breathed out, and squeezed the trigger on the end of her exhale.

Two-tenths-of-a-second later, the turkey's black eye in the middle of its red oblong head displayed daylight through the .22-caliber bullet hole.

Morgan County Correctional Complex, Wartburg

Wayne Fogle—29, clean-shaved head, close-cut goatee, fat on carbs, and tattooed across both upper arms, back, and chest—sat on his cell cot, awaiting permission to make his allotted weekly telephone call.

He quit speaking to his wife Sandra, the physician assistant in charge of the medical aspects of the Madisonville Pain Management Clinic, after she broke a bottle of Colt 45 malt liquor over the crown of his head. Charges were never pressed against Sandra, as the shattering glass fell against Wayne's noggin when he was in the act of choking her as they wrestled in the kitchen. She could have easily picked up an eight-inch serrated carving knife and gutted him. Plus, she'd previously filed an order-of-protection against her husband.

Wayne needed to speak to Leeza Wruck, as his release date approached at the end of the month.

Although he'd sponsored pill abusers for Leeza two years prior to beginning his sentence, she'd publically ratted him out to Monroe County Sheriff Buddy McCoy—who was in on the scam—and Wayne regretfully served his two years to clear his debt with the Wrucks.

Leeza actually killed three pill-business birds with one rat-smashing stone. Wayne fell in line after trying to rip off Leeza by skimming profits and abusing Sandra, but Leeza kept herself insulated from the law by colluding with Buddy and fingering Wayne—a known doctor-shopping, opiate-addict sponsoring other addicts—and thereby buffed the shine on her *legitimate* business. Which legitimized Buddy, as well.

Sandra made the mistake of tipping off Wayne about Leeza's go-to-prison-to-pay-your-debt-plan while he sucked a third quart of Colt. Hence, the choke-out and head-smash. Everyone waited for Wayne to heal before Leeza ratted him out to Buddy and executed the plan.

***

Things hadn't always been so bad between Sandra and Wayne.

She'd first spotted him in the cafeteria between South and North Carrick Halls at the University of Tennessee. He wore farmer's overalls, a holey yellow T-shirt displaying the phrase *Mellow Out*, shoveled food into his mouth with his head bent low, aligning the plate into close range, and smiled a lot, chatting with friends.

She'd approached him at the dessert counter while he grabbed for a piece of carrot cake, and after lunch, they strolled around the commons hand-in-hand, after he reached out and she accepted his paw. As they came to a secluded corner of campus with a line of trees to their backs, they hid in the shade and passed a joint back and forth after Wayne produced it from the lining of his filthy John Deere cap.

Wayne was a sophomore studying math in the hopes of becoming an aeronautical engineer, and he knew he was in way over his head academically. A life-long infatuation with airplanes germinated his aerospace-engineer ambition, but a deficit of math-skills kicked his tail early in the program, so he immediately dialed back the dream, re-considered his major, and sold a little weed to earn free bags of smoke and tamp down the pain of failure.

Wayne's dad owned Worry Free Tire Service, a chain of Yokohama stores scattered throughout East Tennessee, raking in an annual seven-figure net profit, and his folks held plenty of cash. But they insisted Wayne make his way in the world single-handedly—it had worked for his old man, after all. But Wayne hated the tire business and physical labor.

His parents never sent him extra money, except on his birthday, though they paid for his education and living expenses, as long as he maintained a credible GPA. He didn't mind his parents' high expectations; he realized the benefits of thinking big. But parental love remained conditional, dependent upon his latest success, his latest trick. He'd been a high school football standout, and with his head coach also being his math teacher, he'd been able to maintain passing grades due to his prowess with inflated pigskins. But reality deflated his dreams via aeronautical-engineering curricula. Splat!

Sandra, a tall, blonde babe in Wayne's eyes, had said she held high expectations for herself. She told everyone she was five-eleven, but she stood six-feet-tall naked in socks, her green eyes smiling, along with her wide mouth and slightly crooked but gleaming-white teeth. A thin face, high cheekbones, long arms, and shapely legs drew attention from the male-wolves during her mini-skirted walks across campus. Besides a predilection for bad boys like Wayne, her main fault was an obsession with her smallish boobs, something she wanted to fix as soon as funds became available.

She told Wayne that her stepdad couldn't keep his hands off her once she'd reached puberty, and she'd stormed out the door for good upon high school graduation.

She worked as a waitress and a dancer down at Juicy Lucy's to make ends meet, supplementing two scholarships won in high school. The fact that Wayne came from a wealthy family tipped the scales in his direction.

They tangled like springtime muskrats on the bedsprings, Sandra carefully preventing germination of baby Fogles. She was only a college freshman after all, gaining credits to enter nursing school with an eye toward a PA career. No harm in having a little fun between studying, slinging eggs, and shaking bootie bucks. So they hooked up, began dating, and eventually moved in together at the start of summer term.

But when final grades arrived, Wayne had flunked out of the engineering program. Wayne's weed business kept them in rent money, while Sandra put food on the table, clothes on their backs, and gas in the beat-to-death Honda Civic, all while keeping her grades intact.

They married in a civil service at the Knox County Courthouse the summer of her junior year. Neither set of parents attended, since they didn't know. Neither a bridesmaid nor a best man could be rounded up for the quick ceremony, with a pizza to follow at a small restaurant downtown on 16th Street off Cumberland Avenue.

Wayne's parents disapproved of Sandra due to her trailer-park pedigree, no matter her ambitions or achievements, so Wayne kept the betrothal and subsequent marriage mum. Besides, he banked on Sandra's brains and upcoming salary. He'd met Leeza Wruck at Juicy Lucy's, and she'd offered him a sponsorship in the pill business.

Wayne could afford to kiss his conditional-loving parents goodbye. They lived low and didn't enjoy free-flowing loot until Sandra joined the Wruck Empire after winning certification, then combined to rake in fifteen grand a month.

Even with prosperity and all its breathing room, Sandra retained a crazy mannerism. After breast-augmentation surgery, Wayne noticed she constantly monitored her now gravity-defying breasts. Looking in mirrors. Gazing at her reflection in shop windows. Adjusting the rear-view mirror to size up her cleavage. Looking into the eyes of strange men to revel in their wolfishness.

Wayne puffed weed waking-to-sleeping, and ballooned to 270 pounds. She'd nagged mercilessly, and he drank more, swilling down the Lortabs with Maker's Mark, happy-high Wayne morphing from Dr. Jekyll into bitch-slapping Mr. Hyde.

Hence, the two restraining orders. And the final choking out. And the Colt 45 bottle cracking across Wayne's crown.

***

A guard appeared at the barred cell, and Wayne rose to begin his long, foot-dragging slog to the pay phone. "I'm out on the 30th," he said. "Noon."

"That's Sunday," Leeza replied. "I'll send Bushrod over with a car."

"All right, then," said Wayne.

"There's one more thing," said Leeza.

Wayne sat in silence, prison noise shuffling and bickering in the background.

"Sandra's filed for divorce. And you ain't gonna do a thing about it."

Wayne sighed and dropped the receiver, let it swing back and forth on its tangled line, and padded back to his cell as the guard shuffled behind.

Samantha Walker's Journal

Mr. Stephens requires a weekday entry into this diary, even if it's a single paragraph. He lets us coast on the weekends.

Technically, I'm not on probation in the legal sense. But Mr. Stephens knows the depths of my temper, and he *strongly* suggested I participate. He says this journal *may* get me out of jail. You see, I'm still not out of the woods, my babies.

When Bo Wruck intentionally clipped my rear wheel last October as I rooster-tailed Miss Piggy (my Honda motocross bike) toward the finish line, I flipped once in the air and landed on my right side, breaking my collarbone. Pain!

But since I'm left-handed, I could still hold a pencil. Took me six weeks to heal, but I was 100% by the end of Christmas break.

It took me by surprise, you know. The act of writing, even without the hassle of the injury, is weird in itself.

Some days, I ache for it. my emotional guts unwind like rope out onto the page, and all that nastiness wells up and spurts out, and I feel better with the release, like that satisfying moment after a huge dump early in the morning following a spaghetti supper, after you'd ladled on way-too-much hamburger-filled tomato sauce, and that second helping of pasta a big wad-ball the size of Bo Wruck's head, and the next morning, in the middle of the news story about the high pressure fracking and the second cup of coffee kicks in—I've drunk coffee since age six—and you know, it's whoosh! The giant pasta head appears, though this time in darker earth tones, and that little wave of euphoria, a peace, a sense of well-being, floods my emotions, the evacuation of evil sainting me for a full second or two before the hazmat cleanup, two burned matches, and the hand-washing ritual shatters the reverie, and reality meets me outside the bathroom door. Perhaps we'd have less war if everyone enjoyed a good whoosh. I've never met a happy person with constipation.

Mrs. Johnson once said that a talented writer could make a squat sound interesting, so I thought I'd give it a shot. Tell me, kiddies, was it interesting? All we're gonna talk about is crap, anyway, so why not talk of crap literally, right?

giggle

Okay, by now, you might be wondering a bit more about me (picture of the old hag notwithstanding).

Two Army Rangers raised me. My heritage is Cherokee/Scottish, with a mix of Irish and French (warriors, farmers, beaver trappers), and I haven't spent more than an hour in a dress over the course of my entire life. Only at my daddy's funeral.

Amanda Curtis, my best girlfriend, embodies all the wonderful girly-girl traits I lack, wears dresses several days a week, sports make-up occasionally, and will probably join a sorority.

Folks say I'm pretty when I try. But I don't try because Jasper doesn't care. Why pretend when you have your man, and he likes you natural? Plus all that hoop-la about make-up and such? Who has time or the brains for it, really? Not me, certainly not in that direction!

But yeah, Jasper's a bizarre mix. He's an ultra-nerd (his dad is an engineer for the TVA, and a part-time inventor with six patents). And he's a super-jock (plays cornerback on the football team, a head-cracker runners avoid). Kinda makes him an oxymoron, don't you think?

His mother, rest her soul, was an Olympic-level kayaker who lost her life rescuing a kid capsized on the Nantahala River.

Jasper and I've dirt-biked, fished, hunted, hiked, kayaked, and rock-climbed since my dad, Sarge, Ed,

Cornelius, and Alice started teaching us these skills in elementary school.

Why do I always speak about those folks and not others? Like, every kid has two parents usually, right? Well, my biological mom vanished when I was real little. She left, and frankly, I didn't give it much more thought because, hey, she'd wanted out of here, and I wasn't gonna mope over someone who'd clearly not wanted to stick around. Not when I had good folks who'd wanted to look after me all around.

But my grandfather raised me right, with values and a competitive spirit, a love of the outdoors, an acknowledgement of the Big Guy.

And I know that He's not going to make life any easier. That's not the way He works. Life creeps in, as does death, no matter if you're Bill Gates, the Pope, a guy living under a bridge, a pensioner squatting on Hog Holler Road, or Beyoncé. We all catch it. And none of us knows when the hammer's coming down.

But He's there to guide, to lend direction, if I care to listen.

He'll lend a little shade; not enough to sleep under, but enough to rest under before I get up and stumble along.

That's how it works, in my experience, at least, for those willing to kneel down, put their ego aside, and ask for help. A little shade, a taste of manna, and back down the hot path.

This, my babies, do not forget!

Back to Jasper.

Riding bicycles down a Forest Service road back when we were in the sixth grade, Jasper realized I could zoom down the rocky Jeep path faster than he could, that I had slightly better balance, and a whole-lot-less fear of crashing.

Most boys would turn jealous and hit me upside the head with a stick at the realization, but Jasper just smiled to himself and stage-whispered, "A guy with tits!" And he says he's been in love ever since.

It feels pretty weird to be talking about the nature of God one moment, and girl's breasts the next, especially if you're a girl.

There's no good way to say this, Mr. Stephens: "Jasper loves me because I'm a guy with tits."

This is a positive. Because he's describing what I'm not:

1) A blonde in an SUV with a cell phone nailed to her head;

2) An over-painted girly girl who can't see the world beyond her own vanity mirror;

3) A clueless chick living on social media, trying to impress others with a narrow view of her life, carefully Photoshopped to bring out the best and dodge the rest.

Jasper and our friends call that famous social network FaceButt because, instead of revealing your face, you're actually showing your butt. Especially the political stuff. As if you're going to change someone's mind with one more political stab, one more political turd hanging out of your FaceButt. Right.

Amanda showed me a blue banner with white letters, mocking the FaceButt logo, reading: "Being popular on FaceButt is like sitting at the cool table in the mental health hospital."

I bet you're living your whole lives on platforms like FaceButt in your time, my kiddies. Or is that very much a thing of the past, a dinosaur? Maybe social media is the only media and a veritable second life—or *first*, maybe—where you truly exist, rather than the organic, analog life my generation still knows a little about.

Back to the topic. A guy with tits… There's nothing wrong with girly girls, though. Amanda is an absolutely gorgeous girly girl, according to Jasper and every other hot-blooded buck at Kentucky Fried High School. Most men prefer girly girls because The Painted Ones—by nature—shore up male Beta personalities that need more Alpha in their weed-seed-Beta.

Jasper doesn't need any more Alpha, believe me. We don't practice celibacy because we want to; that's a fact. We tried to bust my cherry with a sledgehammer, but it didn't work out.

That's one of those happy accidents people call serendipity. Not that I'm happy about it, though I know it's the right thing to do.

"What makes the desert beautiful is that somewhere, it hides a well," said the Little Prince.

Jasper took 15 years—and we've been around each other since birth—to become my heartthrob, and it scares me that we haven't traveled much or dated others, but I can't deny he's captured my heart.

And in a most unusual way.

Bo Wruck's Journal

Mr. Stephens, you said this journal was only to be read by you, and that you'd burn it when my probation terms are met. Which frees me up to say what I need to say in order to get this pressure off my chest and off my head, both of which pound away like a 650cc single-cylinder thumper with a 13:1 compression ratio, when I think about the daily business, plus school, plus the motocross track.

I don't really give a flip about school, but I can't race in the MX School Boy Division unless I'm enrolled and passing. Blowing the terms of this probation would knock me off the track.

One thing that bothers me about this journal is: who am I writing to? It could be you, but it doesn't feel natural writing to some 59 year-old, balding, amateur head shrinker, whose idea of a good time is picking three chords on a flattop guitar and warbling like a deranged Merle Haggard.

Mr. Stephens, you're an okay guy, and I appreciate the break you gave me to avoid jail in trade for therapy. But you're kinda lame.

If your daddy's Slowburn, and your stepmom is Leeza Byrum Wruck, well, there ain't much left for the imagination.

For example, one day you said that some study concluded that the average American teenage boy thinks about sex every 20 minutes.

I guess we were talking about how to deal with girls at the time.

But I told you that particular research was bull, because me and every other red-blooded male I know thinks about sex every 20 seconds, whether we want to or not. Can't imagine how the coming spring will affect me. Probably like a nitrous oxide shot into the cylinder head—kaboom! I'll be shuffling down the street stiff-legged, making a tent out of my jeans, like I got a 2x4 tied to my thigh.

Sex is so weird!

Think about it. Breasts are basically wads of fat, held up by a few muscles. So if there's not enough fat sticking out of a girl's chest, then the male is not *aroused*.

But if there's too much fat on a girl's chest, like those monster, long, hanging, floppy teats swaying back and forth on Mrs. Johnson's thorax, well, that's a turn-off, believe me.

So this fat-on-the-chest has to be just right, and if this fat can somehow defy gravity and stand up on its own, well, then all the glands are primed just right, and that 2x4 lashed to my leg springs up, and I limp down the road in search of a willing receptacle so millions of microscopic tadpoles can race up a slimy tunnel and impregnate a big egg cell and make a baby.

Unbelievable.

I can just hear that Alpha sperm whispering to that single giant female egg: "Naw, you're not too fat!"

So, yeah, I think it's weird to be aroused by a certain type of fat protruding from a girl's chest, but that must be how we're built, because when Amanda Curtis walks by, her gravity-defying chest fat and that wonderfully built backside with just-the-right-amount-of-fat-mixed-with-muscle—those gorgeous buns fighting like two possums in a gunny sack—well, it causes that 2x4 to instantly spring up on my thigh.

Can't help it.

And to finish, well, it looks like my audience isn't you, Mr. Stephens, or I wouldn't yammer like this. But I have to be writing to someone. Maybe it's myself. Maybe it's the universe. It certainly ain't God, because He ain't listened to me, yet. Elvis is alive, but God's left the building. I wish he was still around, 'cause I can't really trust anyone at the house.

Samantha Walker's Journal

This is embarrassing, Mr. Stephens, but it's also positive, so I'm going to write about it at the risk of being a little-too-intimate, and I trust you'll be faithful to the concept of teacher-student privilege.

We're not supposed to talk about God in school, which is unavoidable, especially at algebra test time, and that's sad. But this is my private journal. My private thoughts.

Anyway, I think He talks to us constantly. We're just too pre-occupied, too self-conscious, too externally preoccupied—think constant texting—to listen.

Here's the best example I can think of, although it happened last fall, right before I cracked my collarbone.

You know that Jasper and I are an item, and that we've been close all our lives. As babies, we rolled around under the kitchen table together, rubbing our snotty noses on the socks of our fathers as they drank coffee and swapped stories around the oak kitchen table. Jasper's mom Alice was always there for me, too, until the day she passed.

My birth mother ran away to God-knows-where, and Jasper's mother drowned when we were 14.

There are way too many people in Kituwah Falls with single parents. But that's the way it is across the entire US.

The debate team and Mrs. Johnson introduced me to the *US Statistical Abstract*, so let's look at the facts:

In 1980, only 19.5% of all households with children lived in single-parent families. But in 1990, it was 24%; in 2000, it was 27%; and in 2008, we're talking 29.5%.

Just for kicks, I looked up the stats for 1960. It said 92% of households had two-parent families. In 1960, about 14% of those single parent head of households were fathers. Now, almost one-in-four are single-father-run.

And then, we talked about the good marriages we knew—his mother Alice and dad Cornelius, Sarge and

Martha, Lois and Pete Shepherd. All strong, positive marriages that spawned good kids.

Maybe our religious background has something to do with it, but we agreed it's a good thing if the two people joining together are doing it for the right reasons.

Which returns me to the fact that God sends messages, and if we're attuned, we can pick up on them and make better decisions. If we're totally into ourselves, our cell phones, our iPods, well. All those natural whispers dissolve, and we're left on our own. Good luck with that.

I read *Journey to Ixtlan* by Carlos Castaneda, which was about this very subject. Castaneda portrayed himself as a rational thinker, but too many unexplainable things happened to him, things he couldn't line up with logic.

And as soon as I finished this treasure—I was sitting in the backyard in a lawn chair at the time—a murder of crows descended out of the forest and landed all over the yard, roosting in trees, on the roof-ridge of the barn, on the clothesline right in front of me. This startled me, because at one point in the book, Castaneda turns into a crow and flies away.

So I ran into the house and called Amanda, because she's going to be an English teacher, and is into symbolism big time. But before I could punch in the numbers, the phone rang.

"Hello, Sam!" Amanda said. She'd had a weird feeling and felt like she should ring me up.

Another time, I was down at the mall, and as I got up to leave, I walked past a car in the parking lot with all its windows down. When I looked inside, what looked like a brand-new iPod sat in the middle of the driver's seat.

Being human, I looked around, and seeing no one, I thought to myself—like everyone else, I get these evil ideas—I can just reach inside and have myself a new Apple gizmo. And just as this thought crossed my mind:

Splat! A big old green June bug smacks me square in the forehead.

Taking a couple of steps back, I blinked a few times and said, "Okay, Big Guy. I get it."

One time, Cornelius was plowing up a couple of acres for a large garden, and Princess—their pup— ran under the tractor. Cornelius was forced to stop. Instead of kicking the dog out of the way, like a Wruck would do, he sat and thought for a minute. Then he walked 30 yards in front of the tractor, and to his amazement, a sinkhole had fallen through, and he would have plowed right into the exposed cave and probably killed himself if he'd continued plowing in that direction. Sinkholes, as you know, are a common phenomenon in Tennessee. There's an underlying layer of limestone in the Southeast, and the water table, which is slightly acidic, gradually eats away at that limestone layer, until one day, a giant hole opens up. If you're unlucky, like that gentleman in Florida a couple of years ago, a state with a similar terra in-firma, you simply vanish. His body was sucked down into the depths, and his remains are now just a product of our collective imagination.

I have lots of examples of this nature-talking phenomenon, and in one case, it's kept Jasper and me from probable parenthood.

Soon after we turned 16, Jasper and I were so in love, the pressure was building to the point where we were going to make a bad decision.

"The eyes are blind. One must look with the heart," said the Little Prince.

I mean, neither of us wants to get married too young, or have kids before we're old enough for the responsibility, or be stuck in a position where we must hold ourselves back academically or professionally.

There's a big world out there, and we want to be part of making it better, which is difficult to do if you're living in a moldy, used single wide with stinky baby diapers a major drain on your $7.45 an hour crap-job with no benefits.

We know kids who've dropped out of high school to have babies, and now pull government checks while complaining about not having enough money to clothe their kids.

What can you do but smile while a teenage mom bitches to your face about the cheap government, with a cigarette dangling out of her lips, a quart of bonded in the freezer, the dad in jail for making meth in the barn, and a second baby twisting inside her stomach, kick kick kicking to get into this crazy world?

Do these folks ever consider the concept of free choice? Hello!

Obviously not.

Here's how it all came into focus for Jasper and me: We knew we were in love, and being hormone-ridden teenagers, we decided to do the deed one time, and then shelf it for marriage.

Right. What a great plan. That's how kids think.

Sarge was away on a forest ranger continuing education course, and Cornelius was deep into some crazy experiment with magnifying glasses, generating electricity with sunlight, and we decided to do what teenagers do.

Of course, Jasper armed himself with condoms, but when we entered the yard, this rabbit sat there watching us. It had a fat brown body with one white front leg. Sitting on the edge of the lawn, Buddha-like, looking right at us. Wagging his fat little head back and forth. Looking at Jasper. Looking at me.

A few minutes later, when I peered out the bathroom window while brushing my teeth, getting ready for Jasper, there was that damn rabbit, looking right at me. Looking like he knew what was up, like he embodied my conscience.

So I ran over to the dining room window and threw back the curtains. There he was. Looking into my eyes.

When I screamed at Jasper, he was lying on the bed in his underwear, waiting. Modest boy.

"No way!" he yelled back.

So I went over to the bedroom window and flung back the curtains to the side yard.

That rabbit sat there on the lawn looking at us, not even blinking. Staring. When Jasper got up to look, the rabbit swiveled its head back and forth, eyeing both of us, just like before, like an evil Chucky doll. Back and forth, back and forth.

The next thing I know, we're rolling around on the bed, laughing our brains out. Then snot actually popped out of Jasper's nose—almost like the churning sperm, it had to go *somewhere*—which tripled the hee-haws.

And then Jasper remembered that Cornelius told him that back in the day, they used rabbits to test for pregnancy. They'd inject the wondering female's urine into a rabbit, and if the rabbit died, she was pregnant. One of the first reliable pregnancy tests.

Jasper and I rolled around the bed laughing so hard, we cried hysterically, and then when the hee-haws burbled out, the realization hit.

We were in way over our heads, and this was the sign.

Damn! Ruined our day.

But that afternoon may have totally changed our lives. Looking into Jasper's big, gorgeous, sky-blue eyes, I knew it hurt him, too, to give up the physical need. At our age, the sex-urge is overwhelming. I'm ready to climb a flagpole and howl at the moon!

And that's a problem with religion, I think. Some people say they're religious, but exhibit other priorities. Adults insist kids practice abstinence, then they don't want you to marry until you're out of college and into your late twenties, early thirties.

What? I'm still trying to figure out these built-in double standards, trying to dig out the good intentions underneath.

But the way it's going, Jasper will be mine, and we'll get married when the timing's right. That may sound far-fetched, but we really love each other enough to hang on a bit longer so it'll last forever.

Listen to the Spirit.

Or not.

Freedom of choice is the one law He never violates. We get to make our own beds. And lie in them.

What makes the desert beautiful is that somewhere, it hides a well.

When the giggles subsided, the tension returned. So we mounted our café racers and wound along the Cherohala all the way to Robbinsville, licked ice cream cones at the Pineapple Whip, kicked rocks in the parking lot, and lazily motored back at a mellow pace, post avoidance.

And that night I dreamed of Jasper and awoke the next morning soaked in perspiration, layered in lubrication, and smiling like a girl whose pee test just came up one stripe short of positive.

Bo Wruck's Journal

I decided that you *are* my audience, Mr. Stephens. For a while there, I was writing to myself, and perhaps I still am. But scribbling this crap is easier if I picture you reading it. Nobody at my house would read anything unless it was a shop manual (Slowburn), a doctor's prescription pad (Leeza), or a skin magazine (Sunny). But he's got porn on the internet now and doesn't need magazines.

Not that I don't like girls. But a bologna sandwich tastes so much better than a picture of a bologna sandwich. Pornography is like sitting in the garage racing the motor in the Escalade. What's the point?

Leeza loves big cars, big homes, big money, so she reads *People* and watches HGTV and QVC a lot. When she's not out beating the roads for business with Lucinda Hornback. They spend a lot of time driving back and forth to Knoxville.

I first started riding motorcycles when we lived in Florida, but it was tough learning motocross because it's so flat there. There are some hills in the middle of the state, and dairy farms. But we lived just west of Tampa, and Sunny and his friends built ramps out of plywood, and pushed dirt up to make little jumps. But that was nothing like East Tennessee, which is heaven-made for motocross.

Not that I believe in Heaven. But if there is one, it's all around Amanda Curtis. Outside of Her Hotness, I don't see any Heaven in my future. Don't even think Sunny and I grew out of the same egg; we're as different as brains and brawn. He's Slowburn's kid all the way. We never knew our birth mom, so I'm guessing she possessed a decent-sized brain, or I wouldn't have landed the lucky egg.

Slowburn says our biological mom overdosed. Imagine that. Can't say I have much feeling over the matter. Never knew her. Leeza's the card I was dealt. And she'll definitely tell me how to play it. We call her the Supreme

Leader behind her back. You already know most of this, Mr. Stephens, but the details are here for your consumption. Since you're the only adult I trust—you've never ratted me out, and you know what'll happen to you if you do—I'll spill my guts.

Because what little I've spilled already lightens the load. I carry this stuff without a word, carried it for years, and it feels good to let a long, strong, brain-fart fly.

Leeza, whom I respect for her craftiness and business sense and ambition, but don't admire much, due to her temper, hooked up with Lucinda Hornback down in Florida. Hillsborough County, land of 107 pain clinics out of the state's 856. They made us read the newspaper in English class down in Florida. They say 46 people OD every day in the US. Now you're making us read the newspaper. Thanks a bunch. But I gots to know my opiates. Killing your customers is one of the negatives, I reckon.

Sunny and I were born in Florida, but Leeza is from East Tennessee. Her daddy, whom she talks about constantly, was a big moonshiner back in the day. Digger Byrum. When the feds busted his operation, he whacked himself instead of going to jail. He was in his early 70's at the time, and not eager to rot in the can. Country boys are like that. Leeza says her mother, Carole, a notorious juicer, passed when Leeza was in grade school. Maybe that's why she doesn't do drugs. All the smart operators avoid that trap. Duh.

Here's the thing, Mr. Stephens: Digger Byrum moved his operation outside of Kituwah Falls to stay one step ahead of the Feds. The business was so big, they were using milk trucks to haul the liquor, and paying off the local cops with hard cash. The heat was too high in North Carolina, with the ATF closing in, so they slipped across the border for a new start. This liquor business, a giant factory-size-still stuck out in a remote holler between

Madisonville and Kituwah Falls, on the edge of the Cherokee Forest, on an abandoned farmstead.

Leeza Byrum met JT Walker—Sam's dad—their freshman year at the same school we now attend, KFHS. This was 1995.

They both loved motorcycles, and she rode on the back of his dirt bike like she was part of the seat. That's what she told me.

Some women just naturally know how to ride on the back of a bike, and that was all it took for JT. Of course, she got knocked up their senior year.

By the time Sam was born, on graduation day of 1998, Sarge was ready to let them get hitched. Sarge wasn't happy about it, but being Christian, he was ready to let them have a go at marriage.

But Leeza slipped out of the room late in the night while the nurses were attending to Sam, and the Florida thing began, with Slowburn and us rug rats—Sunny and me—five years later. Slowburn robbed the cradle marrying Leeza, because she was 23 and he was 41 when they got hitched. They met in a strip club bar, and he was thinking she'd help at home. Wishful thinking. But they've done well business-wise.

Pill-pushing boomed for Leeza and Lucinda all those years down in East Tampa, the endless-trailer-park-opiate-alcohol-hinterlands where we lived. Leeza never spent much time with us, and we pretty much raised ourselves.

Sunny and I realized Slowburn was nothing but a simple Junkyard Dog, when it became clear to us that other people didn't always live the way we lived. Made us tough as nails, though. I can't say I regret my raising, now that it's paying off at the track.

I like having an edge. Sunny, however, could have used a little mother's milk. He seems to be lacking in empathy, a word Mrs. Johnson says means you can relate to other people. His ego ain't his amigo, if you get what I mean. I have an extra-large, double-decker, mega-sized ego myself, which is probably the product of being raised hand-to-mouth and surviving it. But I want to win the war, not just the battles. Sometimes, you've got to rein yourself in and preserve your strength, and strike when it's most effective. Motocross taught me that.

Ask Sam Walker. That cracked collarbone pained her, I know.

Kituwah Falls High School, Conference Room

Reuben Stephens opened the door slowly, and Bo Wruck and Sam Walker entered the empty room and sat in chairs on opposite sides of the table. Stephens placed a half-gallon glass jar of jellybeans between them and sat down.

"You going to juice us up with candy this early in the morning, Mr. Stephens?" asked Bo.

"In a way," replied the counselor.

"I love liquorish best," said Bo.

"Purple for me," answered Sam.

"Y'all know what a metaphor is, don't you?" asked Stephens.

"A place to keep cows," said Sam.

Bo sat with a frown on his face, trying to work out the pun.

Stephens smiled with surprise. *What's a meadow for?* "This is an object lesson," he finally said.

"Our preacher uses object lessons in the children's sermons," said Sam. "It's when you use something physical, an object, to make a point."

"How does Ward Clausen teach an object lesson?" asked Stephens.

"Well, last Sunday, he carried in a pumpkin and said Christians are like pumpkins," she answered.

"I'll say," said Bo.

"How are Christians like pumpkins?" asked Stephens.

"Mr. Clausen said God picks you out of the patch, washes off all the dirt you've collected lying next to other pumpkins, scoops out all the yucky stuff on the inside, carves a smile on your face, puts a candle inside where the gunk used to be, and lights it up for all the world to see."

"That's stupid!" said Bo.

"We're here to work together," said Stephens. "Now you get to sit with me after school for another half hour."

Bo, obviously angered, looked down at the floor.

After a minute of silence, Stephens continued. "My late uncle, Earl Simpson, my mother's oldest brother, taught me the jellybean analogy. He was a coal miner up in West Virginia, and taught mine safety in his later years. To break up the monotony of the safety training, he'd tell jokes, stories, object lessons; anything to keep the men focused, because they weren't accustomed to classrooms, or listening to droning monologues."

"Poo on droning monologues," said Bo.

"One day there was an accident. A worker, eager to please his boss, crawled into an unprotected area, where the coal seam roof hadn't yet been shored up with timbers. This worker climbed under that unprotected roof to retrieve a log chain."

"So?" Bo shifted in his chair.

"So this coal miner ignored safety rules year-after-year in order to please his bosses. Never had an accident. Never had a problem. But on this particular day..."

"The roof caved in and squashed him," finished Sam.

Bo shook his head in agreement, anticipating the climax of the object lesson.

"Exactly," said Stephens. "Every time we take an unnecessary risk, we're eating a jellybean."

"How's a jellybean going to hurt you," asked Bo, "outside of tooth decay?"

"Most of them won't. Most are fine," Stephens said. "The problem, what you don't realize, is that one of those jellybeans is poisoned."

Bo and Sam turned in their seats to look Stephens in the eye.

"Every time you gobble a jellybean, every time you take an unnecessary risk, commit an idiotic act, take a chance holding severe consequences..."

"You increase the odds of eating the poisoned jellybean," Sam finished.

Bo's eyes flared, like a biker with his leather-clad-knees scraping the pavement in the sweepers, with trees flying by like a pine wall, waiting to annihilate him should he chance upon one piece of gravel, one wandering turkey, one open-eyed doe in the middle of the highway, one other biker doing the same thing in the opposite lane, wandering far across the yellow line, around the next curve. The clash of metal and plastic and flesh.

"I've seen you gobble a few jellybeans yourself," said Stephens to Sam.

"You can't race without eating jellybeans," she replied. "But the track has rules. We're all going in the same direction. Most people respect the space of all the other riders. You can't be a motocross champion with a broken neck."

Stephens and Sam swiveled to gaze at Bo, who was still staring at the floor. Sam shook her head, and the dimple in her left cheek deepened with her exasperated smile.

Samantha Walker's Journal

I must admit, Mr. Stephens, that I'm starting to enjoy journaling. I've always liked to write, but had no discipline for it. Too much work. Then this. Like a tap that's been opened, and even when you try to close it, well, the leaky faucet keeps drip-dropping, and the flow just never stops.

Oh, it's easy enough to scribble down a few words, and I guess I could get away with that. But my nature favors perfectionism, a double-edged-trait, for sure, and the work deepens when I go back over it to make it sound right. Nothing is ever right on the first try; we all know that.

But once I force myself to do it every day, it becomes habit. It's addicting, like exercise. When I run cross-country for motocross fitness, the old endorphins kick in about the middle of that second mile, and I'm high as a Georgia pine, a good high. You want more the next day. So, yeah, I guess I know what a junkie feels like. That feeling of euphoria. It calls at you, eats at your heart and soul, begs you to experience more of it, to indulge, to give in, to let go into its arms. Good thing endorphins are everything legal they can be.

Great, I just outed myself as an endorphin junkie. Perhaps I reveal too much, but how am I going to work through all this crap without exposing what I'm thinking? I have to go there, you understand. Take the leap, plunge into those dark depths that sometimes look like a bottomless abyss, a cesspool of everything swirling inside me, things I don't want to touch most of the time. But here I am being forced to tap into it, and you know me; I don't do things halfway, so here I am, plunging in up to my neck and sometimes even immersing myself to the crown of my head.

I'm probably saying things here I wouldn't say face-to-face, because I'm basically an introvert, prefer paper over lip-wagging, prefer a letter over a phone call, like to be by myself in the woods, or with Jasper, when we can go hour after hour without saying a word to each other, but enjoy every minute. And you're not literally there in front of me. That's liberating, in a way. I get to be me, alone, with no one around, and yet, I'm getting it all out to you, same as I would if we'd been together. Which I'd hate for us to be, you know.

I didn't reach this conclusion on my own. Sarge set the stage, teaching me archery, hunting, motocross, kayaking, being out there in the woods alone. He taught me how to be with myself, to need no one else around, to be comfortable with my own thoughts alone. Life experience is now putting the glaze on this tender turkey, so to speak.

Just being around Sarge, hearing the Vietnam stories, the 60's, his years in the Forest Service, the accumulated wisdom of a lifetime. That's accelerated my spiritual growth, showing me a different world, a different view, not keeping me cloistered, but opening my horizons. That, and the fact that I love nature and try to listen to Her.

I'm nowhere near reaching my potential. Hello, still 18 here, with a lifetime in front of me. If 18 were such a big deal, well, 18 year-olds would be running the world, right? We wouldn't wait for 18 year-old youths to gain experience before they can move on up along the ladder of life, corporate, politics, whatever. But I received an excellent start. My heart aches for people like Bo, Sunny, and their buddy, Sean Sizer. They don't have a Sarge-like presence in their worlds, and they must learn good through the example of evil. Ouch. Getting burned in order to learn the nature of fire.

And speaking of evil... In my case, the worst nightmare appears in the form of Leeza. I know how she makes a living; I know how it's affecting Kituwah Falls— four overdose deaths already in the two years they've been here. Too much of a coincidence that they pop up and these start to happen. Do you believe in coincidence, Mr. Stephens? I don't. At least, not here.

I read the papers, and I scan the obits and wonder what everyone must wonder: "If they weren't sick or old, and didn't have an accident, then how did they die?"

How, indeed? It requires very little brains to put two and two together, to be honest.

I can see that folks are stealing off one another, ignoring their children and paying small ransoms for opiates, and that the latest trend is heroin, since the price of street pharmaceuticals is a dollar a milligram, while it's $50 for one oxy. Heroin is more powerful and much cheaper, and now the seller-creeps are mixing it with fentanyl, so it's much more powerful, and equals more death.

These pushers kill us at the rate of 145 per day nationwide by flooding our country with cheap heroin, made mostly in Afghanistan and central Mexico, according to the research from History class. The history of poppy in the Mid-East. Poppy fields thriving in central Mexico now. Didn't realize what all that had to do with US History until I started reading about all the 20-to-50-year-olds *passing away at home*. The British subdued the Indian sub-continent and enslaved China with opium. This is not a new idea. *Nothing new under the sun*, said Solomon.

You've taught us much, Mr. Stephens, and you didn't forget to teach us about all the good things America has done and continues to do. I hang onto that. We help more people than all the other countries combined, and people spit at our name.

And I wonder how we'll turn this Opioid Titanic around before ramming into the pharmaceutical iceberg and scraping a hole down the length of the starboard side.

We can't fill empty souls with pills, pot, alcohol, merchandise, and sugar. But the real question is, how did it get so empty in the first place? What is the root cause? How can a nation so blessed become so hollow?

Bo Wruck's Journal

I've been thinking about your poison jellybean, Mr. Stephens. Makes sense, I admit. I ate handfuls of jellybeans for years, mostly for kicks. Ten feet tall and bulletproof. That's me.

One of the most enjoyable ways to eat jellybeans is to get some guys together, guys with more money than brains, and each of us throws in $50 on a Friday night and we buy an old beater of a car from that shyster up in Madisonville, ancient fart Guy Fowler—you know the one. Bad breath, bad teeth, greasy complexion, cheap used cars, probably stolen.

We drive these crap heaps back to that old abandoned dirt track out in the woods north of town, with the saplings growing right in the middle of the old dirt bowl. We get high on weed and whiskey, and I usually drive. We pile in and run around and around that old dirt track, doing donuts, plowing down saplings as we go, and when the time is right, we all reach up to the roof, place our hands up there, lock our arms, and then I jerk the wheel to the left and bang!

Barrel rolls! We turned an Oldsmobile over seven times once! You should hear the noise inside that car! Screaming and laughing and watching the world spin around and around, sky, trees, dirt, sky, trees, dirt.

Ain't nothing like it. What a rush!

Now that's eating jellybeans with an ice cream scooper.

The strange thing is: I don't seem to care.

Sean Sizer banged his head back in October, blood flying everywhere.

We all laughed our guts out.

Sean didn't seem to be any dumber than before he hit his head, so we just tied a Rambo rag around his noggin until we could take him back to the garage and stitch him up. Turns out Pussycat is pretty handy with catgut and needles. Said he got a lot of practice in Vietnam, though he wasn't a medic. Engineer sniffing out mines. But he got to sew up a lot of soldiers, too. With our business interests, we can't go running to the doctor every time we get cut.

How's your house coming along, Mr. Stephens? Paid off that mortgage, yet?

Samantha Walker's Journal

The jellybean analogy appeals to me, Mr. Stephens. I usually avoid jellybeans, especially the sugary, teeth-rotting jellybeans. But when you're vying for the lead on the last lap of a Moto, jellybeans are too scrumpdillyicious to refuse. And yeah, that rush also helps. Like a little booster addition, if you want.

Sometimes, you have to eat jellybeans, like leaping into a fast river to save a struggling swimmer. But if it looks futile going in, there's no reason for two to die. Alice Whitlock's heroic death taught us that. She probably thought she'd come out all right, though. I guess you don't think about consequences when someone's in danger and you're able to help.

The Whitlocks and Walkers avoid firearm-associated-jellybeans. That's been drilled into our heads from the time we could walk-and-talk. Every aspect of gun safety.

And we're jellybean-free on the highway. Jasper and Amanda make fun when they ride with me in a car or truck; they say I'm an old lady on the highway. Slow, defensive.

When fully suited, armored, helmeted, booted, and astride a well-tuned Honda CRF250R, my blood gets up. I'll nibble my tasty jellybean then.

Bo's another case, however. He seems to relish ice-cream-scoops of jellybeans, and that makes me wonder if there's a death wish under all that bluster. I know life isn't normal at the Wrucks' place.

Sarge and Ed are surveilling the source of the Wrucks' wares. All we know so far is that Leeza and her Camel-fired-whiskey-breath buddy Lucinda Hornback make several laps to Knox-Vegas each week, and the whole Wruck family last resided in Florida, which over the last few years has cracked down on pill mills, driving operators north. They must have slithered into town to escape both forms of Florida heat.

Since Tennessee's lawmakers are slow to regulate opiates, though they're beginning to try, the state's fertile ground for these human cockroaches. They've scurried up here, set up shop, poisoned the community, and raked in fistfuls of cash. You should see the equipment and support Bo has at the track. Full-factory-race Yamaha YZ250F, two backup bikes, all the Snap-On tools you can stuff into a 24-foot enclosed trailer pulled by a monster Cummins diesel Dodge Ram, brand new. Sunny drives a 2011 Corvette to school! He couldn't spell Chevrolet if you held a gun to his head.

Leeza's henchmen, Bushrod Stout and Pussycat Melton, stumble off to Cherokee each weekend and blow thousands of dollars gambling.

Sarge's buddy deals cards at the blackjack table, keeping him apprised.

Slowburn Wruck is the fattest, meanest, stinkiest human cockroach in town, and he just plopped down $60,000 for a Harley trike. That's more than seven times what great-great-grandpa Zeke paid for the farm back in the day.

All through poisoning countless folk in Florida, and now they're salting these hills with oxy, hydrocodone, Lortab, Suboxone, you name it. Kids at school tell me people now abuse Suboxone and methadone, other opiates that are supposed to get you *off* of opiates. Go figure. Are we treating drunks with alcohol now?

I suspect you know how Pain Management Clinics work, since you read the papers and try to piece it all together, the way you taught me. But I'll spell it out here for the future kiddies.

Unemployment is high in Middle Tennessee, just like the rest of the Southeast, so there's no end of willing participants to enroll into their trap. Folks out to make a quick buck on someone else's misery. These people are called sponsors. A sponsor is given $350 from some bloodsucker like Pussycat Melton, the amount a pill mill requires for *treatment*. Then they visit the clinic, turn over the cash, and receive 90 pills. Oxies plummeted in value after drug companies reformulated the mix, so that abusers can't crush and snort them. Oxies have dropped to a dollar a milligram, and come in 30mg or 50mg doses.

So the sponsor returns $2,700 worth of street-value pills to Pussycat, who pays off the sponsor in cash or pills, whatever they want—usually $300 or 10 pills, and Pussycat pockets the rest. Most of the sponsors slink back to their holes and live off the $300, plus whatever the government doles out in welfare.

Sunny and Sean sell pills to the kids at school, while Pussycat and Slowburn supply the adult junkies throughout Monroe and Meigs Counties. Bigger fish on the food chain must have the more populous, more lucrative counties like Knox, Blount, and Sevier, according to Ed.

Bo's the muscle for KFPMC, and Bushrod's the banger for MPMC. You'd think Bo's too young for this work, but Ed says the boy has no problem knocking heads.

Sarge and Trent track these fat possums, and love this type of police work. As you know, Ed lost the 2012 sheriff's election to Buddy McCoy, the pill vote carrying, so we know why the law looks the other way.

Sarge retired from the US Forest Service two years ago, so he and Ed have all the free time in the world to make life miserable for the Wrucks, which worries me. What he's really getting into and all that…

Crooked doctors don't run many of these pill mills. An MD has to sign the papers to be a supervising physician, and Ed says the Knoxville bosses have city doctors on the payroll for this purpose. They never show their faces around the clinics.

The PMC the Wrucks opened in Madisonville is supervised on the inside by a nurse practitioner. According to Sarge, an advanced-practice-nurse can only prescribe controlled substances under the supervision of a medical doctor, but those docs don't have to be on site. Madisonville started out with an MD in house, but when he up and moved away last year, Leeza—the outside manager, the one who keeps the sponsors flowing—kept the clinic open for business because the nurse-practitioner's pain management certificate was still good. That's all they needed, along with that signature from the MD on the payroll. It's complex, but these cockroaches are smart. I have to wonder, however, why the first doctor moved out of town so quickly.

Bo tries to stay out of this mess, I think, because he's focused on motocross. Leeza and Slowburn hold him up as the Golden Boy, which rankles Sunny, who's doing the work, but not hearing the *attaboys*. Unless you count greenbacks as attaboys.

Bo is Lucinda's collections man, so he's connected to the business in a way that forces poison jellybeans down his throat.

But enough about those creeps. Jasper and I concentrate on school first, my motocross second, and recognize the odds of making The Big Time are miniscule. There are virtually no women in the upper echelons of motocross. It's expensive and time consuming. Sarge forks out nearly $15,000 a year to keep me going, and this is the amateur level. Most of my free time in the spring, summer, and fall are spent practicing or racing, while Jasper and Cornelius wrench the motorcycle.

There is a Women's Motocross Association, but it doesn't host enough races or pay enough to qualifiers to make a living with racing. So I do the best I can at this level, and am practical about the next step. University. Bachelor's degree, biology. Medical doctor, rural medicine. I do have a plan, and I will see it through.

There are tons of kids at school who believe they'll grow up to be professional athletes. Right. Some blow off homework so they can shoot more ball; some refuse to read much because they can get a free pass from meaningful classwork by wearing a football jersey. I've heard them brag in the middle of class: *"I don't have to worry about passing. Coach will take care of it."*

But then you see them in their mid-20's, down at the junior college, taking remedial or developmental reading. Driving smoking clunkers to the community college, laughing about the high school nerds they used to hassle. But in reality, the nerds are now studying at the University of Tennessee, getting degrees in computer science, engineering and chemistry. They'll work for Eastman, Oak Ridge Labs, Volkswagen in Chattanooga, or BMW in Greenville, South Carolina, and drive Corvettes, Beemers and Teslas to work.

While the jocks who got away with murder in high school deal opiates to put spuds on the table.

The thing that is important is the thing not seen, said the Little Prince.

Now Bo has all the advantages on the local tracks, but my experience, competitive nature, and natural ability keeps me in contention. Jasper and Cornelius are top-notch mechanics, spotters, and strategists. We can't afford the latest bikes or the newest equipment, but I'm always right up there in the standings. Though I never really knew him, Dad is beside me, whispering in my ear, and the Big Guy never lets me down. Even the broken clavicle, now completely healed, made me a better rider, because now I know what to expect from Bo when I'm leading late in the race.

State Route 68

The 2015 Escalade motored easily along the well-worn path to Interstate 75, where Leeza and Lucinda swung north to I-40 to reach the upper-middle-class suburbs south of Knoxville, tucked between Fort Louden Lake, a manmade reservoir on the Upper Tennessee River, and the interstate, one hour northeast from Kituwah Falls.

Lucinda fired up another Camel, turned her head, and parted her lips on the right to blow smoke against the shotgun-side window, away from Leeza, who checked the dashboard clock to confirm what she already knew: exactly 20 minutes had passed from the stubbing of Lucinda's last cigarette, a routine as predictable as the US Navy's atomic clock. The brown, window-staining-cloud was one reason Leeza traded for a new Cadillac every other year.

Her issues with Lucinda were minor but worthwhile. The binge drinking, the gossip, the flirtation with Slowburn, the fistfuls of fast food, the clattering false teeth, and the hirsute upper lip were little annoyances Leeza overlooked because Lucinda never failed to attract new sponsors, never failed to keep her clinic supplied, never failed to maintain the cash flow. As constant as the Tellico basin fills the Tennessee River. And most importantly, she never failed to keep the heat off Leeza.

Nothing within Machiavelli's *The Prince* or Sun Tzu's *The Art of War* outstripped Leeza's innate ability to manipulate her pawns, outthink her adversaries; a degree of expertise genetically and experientially gathered from her formative years surviving her father's, Digger Byrum's, upbringing.

***

Digger, a fifth-generation moonshiner, operated out of Newport, Tennessee for nearly 30 years, methodically eliminating his competition along the way.

When the ATF, lying outside the local realm of bribery, moved in for a bust, they caught Digger's men hauling hooch out in milk trucks. The underground distillery sat deep in a massive cave carved out by the Pigeon River, where it joins the French Broad. The still was fed by a pure limestone spring, discovered by Digger's great-great grandfather Patrick Byrum upon his return from the Revolutionary War, after he accepted a land grant for flat rich soil—now called Irish Bottom.

Descending from Pennsylvania Irish, the 18th Century Byrums headed south, settling first near Cosby Creek, then in Cocke County. Leeza's great-great-great grandfather Patrick and his son Aiden preceded other Irish settlers in the flats near the French Broad, and many of those newcomers abandoned their limestone-cutting trade to become Patrick's moonshine distributors.

Making headlines with Digger's demise, the Feds pushed for imprisonment, and the long-bearded moonshiner splattered his brains in the back of the cave with his 1911 Colt .45, rather than attend Brushy Mountain Penitentiary.

***

As they pulled into the wide suburban driveway, Leeza marveled at her mentor's self-control. With a $2 million annual income, Odessa Blankenship still chose to live in an upper middle class, unpretentious neighborhood, a well-built but unpresumptuous Cape Cod with four bedrooms, three baths, a two-car garage, and a mere 2,500 square feet of living space.

Her limited and sporadic splurges involved large SUVs, European vacations, holiday parties for her PMC staff, and lavish care, including yoga at Officer on Doody in Maryville, weekly manicures, limo rides in good weather, and organic steaks for her miniature Chihuahua, Buladeen. She flaunted nothing more than a well-heeled-Knoxville suburbanite could afford. Smart.

Thrice divorced, the 55 year-old, slightly obese, highly polished, heavily tanned, bleached blonde drug duchess cohabitated with a Knoxville lawyer, Ron Williams, an ex-prosecutor turned defense attorney, seven years her junior.

"Wait here. I'll be back shortly," Leeza said to Lucinda, who knew the drill. Someone needed to field the iPhone while information was exchanged inside the home, a domicile routinely swept for any electronic surveillance devices. If Odessa carried electronics, the Feds could monitor her, even if the cell was turned off. That's software technology today: Big Brother now monitors targets through dead cellphone speakers.

Lucinda fielding calls from low-level clinic workers posed no problem. They spoke in twangy East Tennessee drug parlance, and exchanged zero information of great importance. If necessary, they employed code. Good doggie = sponsor. Bad doggie = law enforcement. Hungry doggie = pill client. Happy doggie = reliable pill client. Rabid doggie = a cheating pill client needing Bo's or Bushrod's attention.

Odessa Blankenship distributed nearly twelve million pills per year to East Tennesseans through her pain clinics. She'd survived 15 years in the pill-mill business—a dozen in Florida, three in Tennessee—by keeping field bosses to a bare minimum, two counties per captain, and each capo knowing that any breach equaled death. Already, nine (confirmed) customers in the Cumberland Plateau had perished via overdose. Yet, she roamed and ranged and sold and partied and lived as though law enforcement did not exist.

Leeza knew that was the angle she needed to bone up on. Learning from Odessa took time and patience. A true

95

guru would never hand over the scrolls of knowledge in toto. One had to watch, listen, and pay attention. Keep one's head. Attached.

Leeza rang the doorbell while wiping her feet on a smiley face welcome mat. Several minutes passed before the door cracked open.

Odessa, oozing out of a tight red-and-white floral sun dress while juggling the bug-eyed Buladeen— foisting a contentious growl and sniveling upper lip—smiled and led Leeza into a dropped-floor living room, tastefully furnished in dark walnut matching the Craftsman interior woodwork. Yellow maple, smooth pine, or stained walnut comprised the triple-polyurethaned floors, luxurious carpet down only in bathrooms. An oversize Oriental rug drew eyes to the center of the living room.

"You chose not to call on the land line, so there must be something up," said Odessa, who leaned in and whispered, "I wasn't expecting to see you for another couple of weeks."

"Business is great. We've grown at a 20% rate over the last few months," said Leeza.

"But?"

"We've got a couple of bad doggies on our trail," admitted Leeza.

"Do you know these people?" asked Odessa.

"Unfortunately, one of them is Sarge Walker, my ex-father-in-law from another life, plus his buddy Ed Trent, the sheriff we unseated in the last Monroe County election."

"So they both have the hots for you," said Odessa.

"That's one way of saying it," replied Leeza.

"And there must be other people in the loop. These guys have many friends in the area?"

"Bred and born in Kituwah Falls. They have friends scattered from Etowah to Cherokee. Even the blackjack dealer at the casino has their back. Dipstick Pussycat figured that out when the man let him and Bushrod win a few times too often so they'd keep going back."

The walnut grandfather clock in the vestibule ticked loudly for a long minute as Odessa studied her blood-red nails. "An expiration date, then. ASAP."

Leeza nodded.

"Let's get it done before Memorial Day," Odessa said. Buladeen squirmed in her arms and growled. "These men are veterans, you say?"

Leeza nodded again, smiled, showed herself to the door, and shut it behind her. She opened the driver's door just as Lucinda terminated a cell phone call.

Lucinda nodded toward a Silverado parked four houses down the street, and Leeza smirked as she pulled out of the driveway, shook her head, and drove away.

Juicy Lucy's

Leeza and Lucinda sat at the bar, as far from the dance stage as possible, sipping double whiskeys and talking business each time Stan, their favorite bartender and Odessa's vigilant stool pigeon, worked the other end, the blare from the house PA masking their conversation.

"How'd you ever get hooked up with Slowburn?" asked Lucinda. "He's so much older, and a…" she let her words fade into the blaring disco music.

"Slob," finished Leeza. "He wasn't always a slob. When JT and I ran together back in high school, Slowburn was back from the military and doing well peddling tea and acid with Pussycat and Bushrod, and he was pretty hot, actually. All muscle and easily…" She let her words drain into the background noise.

"Manipulated," finished Lucinda.

"Well," continued Leeza. "When Daddy moved back to the mountains to keep his shine business going, I hooked up with Bushrod there because he fit the bill with what I was trying to accomplish at the time. It ain't exactly a first-rate romance," she mused.

"Came with some baggage, too," said Lucinda.

Leeza's eyes squinted through cigarette smoke as she fought down her anger. "Those boys are sure helping us out now, though," she countered.

"Can't deny it," agreed Lucinda. She surveyed the naked dancing girls and said, "Most of these dancers are college girls putting themselves through school the best they know how, same as I would."

"No, you wouldn't," said Leeza with a smile.

"I was skinny back then." Lucinda laughed.

"I'll take your word for it," said Leeza. "How's the clinic in town going?"

"Great. That girl I hired a year ago, Kristen Burley, is a natural businesswoman," said Lucinda.

"Yeah, my girl Sandra Fogle is kick-ass, too. Drafted her right out of college when we moved up here. It pays to do your homework and vet these new hires. But most of the pill heads would buy opiates from cigar store Indians," said Leeza. "Sandra's always coming up with great ideas. Yesterday, she suggested that when we hire new help, they should all be legitimate. We're already mixing legitimate customers in with the skimmers, but that would only help the overall appearance of legitimacy."

Lucinda slugged back her Jameson and bent to hear better.

"She calls it the buddy system. You pair up the skimmers. One goes in and gets pills, like always. But the other gets their blood pressure checked, or some ordinary procedure," Leeza explained.

"And the next week, they change roles, making the records look more legit," Lucinda interjected, finishing the thought for Leeza.

They slapped a high five, waved Stan over, ordered two more double whiskeys, plus shots of Patron on the side.

"Y'all can knock it back," noted Stan.

"Practice," said Lucinda with a trailing cackle.

Stan smiled and walked to the opposite end of the bar.

Lucinda asked, "How'd Sandra come up with that?"

"The State of Tennessee finally woke up and created a database of prescription users, according to Odessa." Leeza blew a long plume of smoke at the ceiling, the colored lights filtering the haze red and blue. "I asked Sandra if she could figure a way around the database. A couple of days later, she unfolded her plan," continued Leeza. "I ran it by Odessa, and she okayed it. She said to swap paperwork with our clinics down in Georgia, which will water down the evidence."

Another high five, and shots of Patron down the hatch.

"Let's move on those three dopes near the stage," said Lucinda. "Time for action."

Leeza followed after ordering another round, plus three more whiskeys to be carried to the small table in front of the college girl shaking her ample university-cafeteria-fed backside in the faces of the sodden salesmen blowing off steam from a 60-hour work week, nearly paralyzed on Fort Louden Pain Management Clinic Vicodin. Feeling no pain at all.

One of the dopes, Harry Weems, a handsome sandy-redhead with fading freckles and athletic build, immediately hit it off with Lucinda.

At first, she giggled like a schoolgirl at his jokes, annoying Leeza. But when Lucinda made no effort to remove his hand from her upper thigh, Leeza threw her the stink eye.

Lucinda ignored Leeza's negative signals, spent the night with Harry, and acted bubble-headed about him the next day at their early afternoon Bloody Mary lunch.

"So who is this guy? Where's he from? What's he do?" Leeza fought back black intuition, winced under a raging headache, and tried to fake interest in Lucinda's new buddy Weems.

Lucinda shrugged. "Don't rightly know," she giggled, losing herself in vodka and two desserts, smiling quietly to herself.

Kituwah Falls Pain Management Clinic

Fair-skinned Harry Weems, 42, pulled into the parking lot and sat for a long moment watching customers dribble in from the apartment building next door, which served as the holding area for addicts and skimmers waiting patiently to fill prescriptions.

A wolfish grin spread across his face when he realized the killing he could make on the lambs inside.

The Hot Springs, Arkansas native first made his way to East Tennessee in 1995, accepting a job in a Knoxville clinic as a radiologist after earning an associate degree and radiologic technology certificate from National Park College.

The low pay and boring repetition of radiology soon frustrated him. When a friend on Harry's amateur softball team suggested that he "sell those damn machines instead of running them," he put his resume in with a Japanese firm specializing in the production of high-dollar medical-optical equipment, and to his surprise, they hired him after a series of interviews. Weems found himself two months later in Atlanta, Georgia, selling CT scanners and MRI machines to large hospital chains, his good looks and natural charm paying off.

Harry's salary jumped from 25k to 50k, but he stashed most of his income in savings, stock, and new condo payments in a gentrified neighborhood. The son of middle-class shopkeepers, Harry knew how to bleed a buck, but he also yearned to leap ahead when opportunity arose.

In 2001, he earned promotion to regional sales manager, and his paycheck jumped another notch to 75k. Living in Atlanta was expensive, but his habit of using women instead of marrying them grew the savings-investment-cache until his company sold out and Harry suddenly found himself jobless post-acquisition.

101

So he sold the condo and moved back to Knoxville, rented a cheap apartment near the university, took up with his old buddies still hanging onto the amateur softball social circle, and laid low, waiting for opportunity.

The same buddy who turned him on to the idea of medical equipment sales those many years ago hoisted a fresh idea. Pain clinics.

Since Harry's background was in the medical field, he immediately did his homework, scouted out, then dated a nurse in Odessa's Fort Louden shop, and soon learned that this pill-pushing-pot-of-gold held no bottom.

But he also learned through the chatty nurse that Blankenship ran a tight ship, and no outsiders invested in the business. Odessa controlled the whole wad while her mate Ron Williams greased the local authorities. They'd pocketed one circuit court judge, one criminal court judge, and two prominent Knoxville MD's.

Lucinda and Leeza moved on Harry at Juicy Lucy's, so he immediately jettisoned the nurse and focused on Lucinda, an easy mark. It was obvious that few men suffered that horse face, cigarette breath, greasy-lipped-gluttony, and foul mouth. And she sat deep in the Blankenship Empire.

Disgruntled.

***

Ron, a long-time business associate of the Cubans, hooked up with Odessa during her last two years in Tampa. The happy couple enjoyed common-law marriage status following nine years of cohabitation and residency in three states.

A first cousin to Ernesto Lemus, Ron was taller than most, fit, and powerful—intimidating lesser lawyers poised against him in the Knoxville Circuit Court. His shining black eyes, golden skin, gleaming capped teeth, and $5,000

Armani suit rounded out the perfect picture of a savvy defense attorney, suggesting to his rivals they'd encountered the Prince of Darkness himself.

Ron's mother was Ernesto's aunt, and the first cousins shared many qualities, including a long memory for anyone standing in their path.

Ron's Cuban features favored the Negroid blood of the island's racial mix, and several times during their early Jesuit school years in Miami, he and Ernesto had ball-batted junior high school white, aristocratic bullies, ignorant of their spontaneous tempers. Word of their physical boldness and propensity for swift attack rendered their high school days pacific.

An ambivert, Ron was as comfortable holed up in his $80,000 man-cave as he was in full regalia, pursuing the law before a courtroom audience.

Ron revealed himself as an Epicurean narcissist early on in his relationship with Odessa—constantly challenging her sense of fidelity with frequent holidays from monogamy. But now, the required eight-years-of-conjugality had passed, and legal boundaries fell around them. Ron settled down and left Juicy Lucy college girls alone.

Perhaps opiates wet-blanketed Ron's testosterone-levels, as well. Odessa kept him covered in pills, cash, weed, and cooked rich meals at gourmet levels while he provided legal defense for the PMC chain as payback.

Slowburn Wruck's Garage

Slowburn. Pussycat. Bushrod.

Three amigos, three stooges, wrenching old cars, hopping up motorcycles, racing down highways, mooning folks out the side windows, playing loose women, drinking, selling weed, pills, cheap heroin to those unable to afford the rising price of opiates.

Slowburn's a weed man. Dawn to dusk. Suck and exhale. Roll, fire up. Suck and exhale. Day in, day out.

Bushrod's a pill man. Vicodin. For the knees, of course.

Pussycat can't handle smoke, speed, or oxy. Makes him fuzzy. Only one thing crystallizes his thoughts.

Juice.

Pussycat begins the day with a water glass of whiskey. Gets them engines rolling. Sips all day, half the night. Pass out. Repeat.

The garage is their haven, their soiled-stinky-heaven, their solitary-blood-brother-Raccoon-Lodge of never-ending bullshit hosting boasts and life-long-camaraderie.

They sit, spit, drink, chew, smoke, gossip, wrench, harass one another, plan and conspire. Take turns racing Bo's moto bike up and down the road, never up into the hills, requiring clear-headed finesse, wrenching kinks out of the Yamaha, setting-up tires, and tuning for the quirks of the next track on the circuit.

"What we gonna do with them fellers tracking the women?" asked Pussycat, turning his head and spitting a long stream of tobacco juice onto the cracked cement floor, a line of brown spittle clinging onto his chin. He took a long pull off the half-empty fifth.

"Same as we done the rest," said Slowburn.

"Walker and Trent got friends all over these counties," said Bushrod.

"We was smart about all the people we've had to handle," said Slowburn.

"None of them fellers was Army Rangers," said Bushrod. "Both of these bastards can hide in the bush and you'd never know they's out there."

The trio traded stares, then hung their heads. Pussy spat another stream between his paint-speckled shoes, wiping his chin with his bare forearm. His mind wandered back to Binh Long firebase, 1968, where he watched rangers return from the bush after a month-long-mission, resupply, and then vanish the next morning before dawn. He remembered the time Bushrod picked a fight with a wiry, mid-sized ranger in a Saigon titty bar. Old Bush now buys Polident on a regular basis.

"Remember that gang initiation thing back at Fayetteville?" slurred Pussycat.

Local black thugs in Fayetteville had hatched the brilliant plan to cull prospective members, making sure only the toughest kids became Crips. Wannabes had to hang in front of Wal-Mart, waiting for the first blond male to walk out, bags-in-hand, then publically beat whitey in broad daylight and win Crip-hood on the spot.

Two Crips generals parked illegally at the front door on the grocery side. An 18 year-old wannabe jumped out and swaggered up-and-down the sidewalk, waiting for his victim. The first three people out the door? Geriatric women. Hags. Two minutes later, a six-foot California surfer dude ambled out with a small bag of apples in one hand. Sunburnt blond hair.

Muscly looking, straightedge, Springsteen-loving, smiley-faced Surfer Dude.

The wannabe pulled his pistol and turned to smash the butt down on the man's head, but Surfer Dude simultaneously dropped the apples, reached up, and grabbed the thug's wrist before he could swing his arm down.

The two gang leaders winced when the wrist snapped and the bone erupted from their boy's forearm. The blond used his second hand to grab the poor kid's crotch through thin-red basketball shorts and yanked both testicles loose.

The kid flew screaming through their windshield, spraying them with glass and blood.

Their intended victim had just graduated from ranger school.

Slowburn. Pussycat. Bushrod.

That was all the soldiers at Fort Bragg talked about for a week. The look on those gang thugs' faces. The crushed windshield, like a cradle for that youngin'. The car zipping away with the kid kind of attached.

"You can't make that shit up," sighed Bushrod.

"No. And we can't play half-ass with rangers," said Slowburn as he dropped a smoking roach into an empty Pabst can and smiled at the sizzle.

Bo Wruck's Journal

Amanda Curtis just strolled by the window with her long legs and mini-skirt. But Sunny and Sean Sizer chased right behind her, and I can tell they're up to no good. The way they sneak around, slouchy shoulders and all, talking trash.

Sean's family is a head-trip. There's eleven of them down there in that falling down shack on St. Louis Street. The place is a marvel to behold. Shutters hanging off the hinges, green mold all over the vinyl siding, gutters overflowing with sticks and tree crap. The yard is rubbed raw down to the dirt from the constant tread of kids and farm animals.

I made the mistake of going down there last week to find Sean. Pussycat needed some help changing a truck tire, and I don't lower myself to lifting heavy objects, unless I'm training for motocross. Don't want to sully my hands with greasy tire gook.

Anyway, I go down there and Sean's fat mom, Sylvia, is standing in the kitchen wearing a torn, faded green housedress with dried food, coffee spots, and grease all caked on the front of it, with the backside all stuck up in the crack of her butt. Scabs all over her legs. A couple of kids hanging on to her knees with *green elevens* on their upper lips. You know, that greenish snot coming out of both nostrils.

Lamb legs. Yikes!

She asks me if I want a cup of coffee, but when I look at a cup that's on the counter, there's a couple of dead flies floating. Sometimes, I'll fish a fly out of my beer if they're still swimming. Don't want to waste a good beer. But this?

"No, thanks," I say.

I notice she's cooking supper, but there's only one pot holding a rump roast in there.

She says, "You know why they call it a rump roast?"

I say, "I dunno."

She says, "Because no one would eat it if they called it cow's ass." Then she starts cackling like the Wicked Witch of the West.

Ass ain't a bad word is it, Mr. Stephens? They tell me it's used in *The Bible*. There's even a talking ass in *The Bible*, according to Sam Walker, the know-it-all. She said this ass in *The Bible* asked its master why he was whacking him with a stick. Balaam was the man's name. He was whacking the ass with a stick because he couldn't see an angel blocking the road. But the ass could see the angel. They must have had some great wacky-tobacky back in Bible days, Mr. Stephens. Pure organic!

And I know the word ass is all over the place in *Aesop's Fables,* because they made us read them in grade school. Most of them stories use ass as a substitute word for people. I know Aesop's talking about people when he tells ass stories. You don't have to be no English major to figure that out. People are asses, that's easy to see. A natural connection.

Some people are ants, some are grasshoppers, some are asses, and some are snakes. It's all right there in *Aesop's Fables.* Ancient folks seen it all before. "*Nothing new under the sun*," says smarty pants Sam Walker. Teacher told us Aesop was a black slave back in the Greek days, which makes sense to me. Had that slave perspective. Could see folks for the asses they were.

Sylvia stabs the rump roast with a big butcher knife and plops it directly onto the kitchen table, no plate or nothing. Then she yells in this screechy voice, "Come and git it!"

All these kids flock in like birds and start pulling off pieces of rump roast and stuffing them into their mouths. Tough luck for the kids still out in the yard or down by the creek.

Right then, I happen to look up at the light fixture. Way up on the pull chain, there's a tiny mouse skeleton dangling. Ain't no meat left on its bones, so I know it's been hanging there quite some time.

Truth's stranger than fiction, and I ain't read but little fiction, but if you make up stuff like this, people'd say you was telling a stretcher.

But there's more. I felt a little weak in the stomach, so I walked into the next room and Ted Sizer, the old man, is in there with a hand ax, chopping carpet. Not a knife or a box cutter. A hand ax.

It's been a bit wet and nippy for March, not hot and dry like last year, and their nasty old brown carpet was over a big hole in the floor where the register used to be. They burn coal for heat and throw the clinkers down on the road. You ain't lived until you've fallen off your bike and scraped your knees across some clinkers. That's what one of the Sizer kids told me. Cute little kid with dirt smudged on his face and a hole under the gaping arms of his XL Budweiser T-shirt draped over his whole body like a body bag.

So Ted's chopping a hole in the carpet with his hand ax, down on his knees, and on his feet are old muddy boots. The Sizers have a few scrawny goats in the back lot, they can't feed them much, and they've already munched the grass down to dirt, and Ted must have been out there earlier, because it wasn't really mud on his boots. Black little smooshed pellets. This didn't help my stomach none, so I went back outside and there was Sean, taking a whiz against the walnut tree. Right out in the open.

There's more. A kid at school, Harold Ramsey, told me he was over there one day before they put that gnarly carpet over the register hole, and he accidentally fell down through the hole when he and Sean were pushing each other around.

While Harold was stuck down there, old 300-pound Sylvia comes over, straddles that hole to see who's down in the dank yelling, and Harold looks up through the bottom of that skanky housedress and starts to gag. He said it burned when that gag stuck in his throat. Then she reached down, took his hand, and pulled him out. Harold said the barf was foaming on his lips, but he never upchucked.

The thing that struck me most about that house was the smell. A mix of sweat, grease, mouse death, cigarette smoke, farts, and kids that ain't been washed proper in months. I think the windows are stuck shut. Maybe nailed down, I didn't look. They ain't never open, that's for sure.

Anyway, I know for a fact that Ted and Sylvia are both pill heads 'cause Lucinda tries to keep them in groceries if they go down to the pain clinic and get them Lortabs using the $350 seed money. They each get $350 worth a month, but they don't buy groceries with the extra pill money Lucinda hands over. Sean told me.

They keep part of the Lortabs, or buy them on the street if Lucinda insists on them taking groceries. Eat them like your jellybeans.

They run out of Lortabs about the second week of the month, so the government check they get for all them kids goes for more dope, about $10 a pop. They still can't make it to the end of the month, and things get real interesting around the 19th or 20th. Lots of screaming and punching and crying and butt kicking. Them kids know better than to be underfoot when the end of the month rolls around.

I don't feel so bad about making money off them. Some of it ends up going toward my motocross racing, and they'd get them pills from somebody else if Lucinda wasn't around.

It's the kids that worry my sleep.

Does that make me weak? Does giving some of those older kids part of my lunch every day make me a pansy? I hope not. I just got to get good sleep or I can't concentrate and race well. My mind just ain't clear if I start thinking about them.

Maybe you can get some of them church folks to help feed those Sizers. That's the only reason I told you all this. And for you to keep an eye on Sean and Sunny. This ain't ratting them out. It's for the Curtis girl.

Now Amanda's walking back in the other direction, and there's tears on her cheeks.

I'll knock their heads together this afternoon, soon as I'm free.

Kituwah Falls High School Parking Lot

Bo folded his journal and carried it down the hall to Mr. Stephens's office after the end of the school day bell rang. Stephens thanked him for keeping up with his work, and Bo nodded acknowledgement before stepping back into the hallway.

Reaching the parking lot, he ran into Jasper and Sam. They nodded and smiled, exchanging no words. Sam smacked a quick kiss on Jasper's cheek, then turned on her heel and headed toward the locker room to dress for cross-country practice.

As Jasper and Bo packed motorcycle saddlebags with books and backpacks, a muffled scream filled the air from the direction of the dumpster in the back of the parking lot next to the woods. The boys looked at each other with furrowed brows.

"What the?" mumbled Bo before dropping his backpack and running behind Jasper to the dumpster.

When they reached the deeply shaded space between the woods and the rust-green metal dispenser, they witnessed Sunny, Sean, and Amanda writhing in the dirt, the girl struggling underneath Sunny, while Sean fought to keep his hands over her mouth.

Jasper flew through the air, knocking Sunny onto his back. Then he rose, picked up Sunny by the throat with his left hand, and shattered his nose with a right-hand-haymaker. One kick to the groin with a booted foot and Sunny swooned to the dirt.

Bo smashed Sean between the eyes, then the steel-toe of his motorcycle boot snapped Sean's head back, shattering his nose, and rendering him unconscious.

Jasper helped Amanda onto her feet as other kids arrived, some boys guarding Sunny and Sean, some girls swarming around Amanda. As Mr. Stephens covered her with his brown corduroy jacket and began talking in soothing tones, Bo punched 911 on his cell.

Sarge arrived ten minutes later in the chartreuse EMT rig, a menacing look on his face. After leading Amanda into the back of the emergency vehicle, he sighed with relief seeing she'd escaped physical injury.

Shaking and crying, Amanda confirmed they hadn't broken any bones.

When Sheriff Buddy McCoy and Deputy Fred Davis pulled up, Walker visibly shook as he reluctantly turned over the incipient rapists, knowing they'd walk before spending the night in jail.

But before Leeza's pigeons hauled them off, he roughly set their noses after cleaning off the coagulated blood with raw 90% alcohol, jerking them up by the chins, and applying bandages with a slap.

That evening, Judge Jubal Plunkett released the boys to their parents, finding insufficient evidence to bind them over to a grand jury on the charge of attempted rape.

Knowing the Wruck gang's reputation in the community, Amanda reviewed her situation with Reuben Stephens privately back in his office amid sobs intermingled with white-knuckle anger, but in the end, she refused to press charges in the heat of Judge Plunkett's intense questioning about her dress and character.

The Cracker Barrel, Maryville

Lucinda sat dreamy-eyed, sipping coffee across the table from Harry Weems, who smiled back between peeks at the menu.

"I'll have the Country Boy Breakfast," Lucinda said to the waitress. "Eggs over easy. Country taters with gravy. Pork chop. Make sure it's fresh. The last time, it was all dried out."

Pig, thought Harry, smiling.

"Same for me," he said aloud. "Except a medium steak instead of the pork chop."

After Lucinda sucked down her plate and longed for a cigarette, Harry nibbled through his meal and revealed The Plan.

"I know you're doing pretty well at Kituwah Falls," he said. "But you know the business so well, and Blankenship seems to wall you off. Ever thought of starting your own clinic?"

Lucinda nearly choked, but recovered quickly and said, "Leeza and Odessa would freak out."

"Probably," said Harry. "But Odessa appears to favor Leeza at your expense."

"Odessa makes me sit out in the car while she goes over business with Leeza," said Lucinda. "Then Leeza has to repeat Odessa's orders on the way home."

"Why?" asked Harry.

"I'm not sure," said Lucinda. "Maybe they're keeping me in the dark for some reason."

No shit, thought Harry. Then he said aloud, "You don't have to stay in the dark with me. Let's start our own PMC."

Lucinda flushed, then said, "We don't have that kind of cash or connections."

"I do," said Harry. "In fact, I have the building and office nearly set up outside Kituwah Falls, on Highway 68, halfway to Madisonville, in an old refurbished gas station."

Giggling, Hornback arose from the table, wiped red-eye gravy from a hairy upper lip with her right sleeve, threw her arms around Harry, and planted a loud wet kiss on his greasy lips while the restaurant audience smiled and returned to their eggs.

Samantha Walker's Journal

I enjoyed your AP History class today, Mr. Stephens. I'm all about science, but this history thing is firing up brain cells, as well.

I didn't know much about US History past the Civil War. Every year, our elementary school teacher would say the same thing: "This fall, we'll start with the Pilgrims." I know more about the Pilgrims, Pocahontas, John Smith, Plymouth Rock, and Ann Bradstreet than I ever want to know.

When we returned to the classroom the next fall, the new teacher would announce: "This year, we're going to start with the Pilgrims."

No wonder nobody understands the direction the country's been heading for the last 60 years, since that political war in Korea.

What you've taught us about the Vietnam War is fascinating, and it explains much about Sarge, too. Also, the fact that Vietnam was invaded *eight* times, and that the Vietnamese people repelled the enemy *eight* times, was an eye-opener.

Chinese, Burmese, Korean, Japanese, Mongolian, and French invasions; all for nothing.

But we thought we were different; oh, yes. We're going to kick some tail in Vietnam! Save the world from the Domino Theory!

Yet, we fell into the same hole. Multiple times. Hindsight is supposed to be 20/20, but I guess others' hindsight is never our own; we're gonna bring about a different outcome. Because we are invincible. We have right on our side. We might even bring God into it, if we're feeling really hyped.

I read last week that Vietnam is now the most-visited destination for vacationing millennials. Sons and daughters of Vietnam vets now visit this openly communist country that happily dabs its feet in capitalism!

The military-industrial complex raked in a few billion off Vietnam. Casket makers profited like bandits. Chemical companies like DuPont cranked out the Agent Orange.

My dad's casket cost $2,300 in 2003. The average price of a casket in 2016 is $5,180. Do you think the average soldiers' pay has more than doubled? I read that the rate of a soldier's deployment has quadrupled since the War on Terror began in 2001.

Hitler had Napoleon for an example, but he got sucked into Mother Russia just the same. The Russians let the Germans roll all the way across the plain into the area around Stalingrad, now Volgograd, west of the Ukraine, on the Volga River. Then winter hit. January-March, 1943. The Russian Army kicked German butt in the largest battle ever fought on Earth. Germany never recovered, and the end of WWII was set.

So we thought we were different from the previous Vietnam invaders. It didn't matter that *eight* invasions were repelled. We were going to win!

One of Sarge's favorite songs is Roger Water's *The Bravery of Being Out of Range*. The lyrics are great, but the video images are frightening. People sitting in bars, hoisting beers to cheer on missiles so accurate, the Air Force was putting them down chimneys.

There's always two sides to every story. But Sarge was *there* in Vietnam. My daddy was *there* in Afghanistan. It's difficult for me to discount prime sources, though what Dad said filtered through Sarge.

You can't talk about this stuff at school. They all think I'm a dweeb, a super-freak, and a nerd.

It's true! I don't deny it; I'm actually proud to be all that!

But all they want to do is stare at their iPhones, jabber endlessly about pop culture, Kanye, Miley, Kardashians,

Caitlyn Jenner. He ordered store-bought boobs, but kept his wanger.

Sports are big, too. Not cross-country or motocross. They're way off to the side of the big money and constant chatter. Football is the number one sport around Kituwah Falls, Madisonville, and the Sweetwater area. Friday nights, Saturday afternoons, and, of course, Sunday are all about football, from August until the Super Bowl. I like watching the games sometimes, if we're playing a rival, or if we're in contention at the end of the season. But the constant football talk numbs my brain.

I actually heard a college football player say this on TV after winning a close game: "Coach says we score more points, we win."

Seriously.

I had to grow up faster than most kids, not having a mom. Raised by men who read and wrote and debated topics over beers Friday afternoon. Not that there aren't smart women out there. Your wife Jewel is a prime example, Mr. Stephens. You're lucky to have someone you can engage in healthy conversation. We've got Elon Musk with Space-X, Jeff Bezos with Blue Origin, and Richard Branson with Virgin Galactic, doing all these terrific things with rockets and space exploration, and we're talking about who's supposed to pee in which bathroom. What? Blows my mind!

Jasper and I haven't enjoyed sex, yet. But *Song of Songs* brings me to my knees, and I crawl into the cold shower after a few paragraphs. I can't imagine sex lasts long. I'm afraid Jasper would last about 30 seconds.

Let's say Jasper and I were enjoying sex. When those short minutes are over, what do you do? Most folks probably roll over and turn on the football game, or *Housewives of Dallas*.

At least Jasper and I can talk about stuff. We talk about our futures. Or just go riding our dirt bikes up on the forest roads, and not talk at all. Kayak down the Nantahala with trout canes.

I can't imagine not having an intelligent person to talk to when my head needs straightening. Maybe that's why folks get paralyzed from the face back on pills. No thought required.

I read in the *Johnson City Press* that Tennessee's getting $3.4 million over the next four years from the CDC to prevent prescription drug abuse. "This scourge affects 5% of Tennessee residents. We're losing more than a thousand Tennesseans a year to drug overdoses," said US Representative Lamar Alexander. We rank third in the nation for prescription pill abuse, and 12th from deaths resulting in opiate overdose. There are 17 states where more people die from prescription drug overdoses than car wrecks or any other form of accidental death. Our state's death rate from overdoses nearly tripled since 1999.

The latest figure I read from the CDC in Atlanta was 29,467 dead from opiates and heroin in 2014. Divide that by 365, and you get 81 per day. Every day.

And that's just opiates. Mix in weed, meth, alcohol, and bath salts. Well. Some kids put paper bags over their heads and snort Pam. The stuff you spray on pots so meat won't stick to them. Amanda said her cousin huffed Pam and cracked his head on the kitchen table heading toward the floor after he blacked out.

Dealers like the Wrucks are responsible, for sure, but who's writing prescriptions? The editorial ends with this: "Physicians who are convicted of operating pill mills should be treated as harshly as those sentenced for fraudulently obtaining prescription drugs under TennCare."

You think?

Bo Wruck's Journal

Me and Sunny are always getting into these fights. Even as little kids, busting up the living room, scarring the walls, breaking furniture, pouring cereal down behind the couch cushions, sticking the cat's butt in each other's faces, riding the dog around the room like we was cowboys, braining each other with cap pistols.

When I heard that a meth lab smells like cat pee, I could relate. We drove through West Memphis once on our way to a motocross race last year, and the whole town smelled like a cat's butt.

"How you know what a cat's butt smells like?" asked Slowburn from the driver's seat.

Leeza and Slowburn didn't seem to care much that we tore the house up. Guess it's hard to tell, the way we live. We've got so much cash, we'd just move every year or two, and let the new owners deal with it. We're kinda like salmon swimming upstream.

Today, I started thinking about weed, Sean's business. Adults in these parts get all upset about weed. A person grows a pot plant and they go to jail, but you can buy that synthetic chemical weed off the internet all day long. After several years of watching folks freak out and jump off bridges and murder their children when they're high on that bath salts crap, the state finally outlawed what's sold in head shops. The Chinese make that chemical synthetic weed out of God knows what, probably toxic chemicals, and dump it on our society.

That brain-cooking synthetic grass is still available because as soon as we write laws prohibiting it, the Chinese mix a new batch of chemicals that don't fit the legal description, and then sell the new crud. Here're some of the names for this gunk: spice, K2, fake weed, Yucatan Fire, Skunk, Bath Salts, and Moon Rocks.

All the while, Mother Nature is illegal. Scientists now say Mother Nature prevents Alzheimer's. No kidding. It keeps down brain inflammation, scientists say. Brain inflammation ain't good for Alzheimer's, they report, and weed knocks down that inflammation because it crosses the blood/brain barrier real easy, and somehow it deadens the inflammation.

Here's the final kick in the pants: about the only place you can get good Mother Nature these days is in the schoolyard. Just ask Sean Sizer. He's got a pot field up in the Cherokee National Forest. He can't grow marijuana in that goat yard. Sunny rides him up the mountain on the back of our four-wheeler after school, and they tend to it. They won't expose the location, and I don't want to know. All the law and the public's worried about kids smoking weed, and the kids are the ones making a buck off it. The adults here are mostly into pills, because that's legal.

This is one crazy, mixed up, ass-backward planet, Mr. Stephens. Kinda makes me anxious to get up in the morning and see what new craziness has reared its head.

I don't see no need in reading fiction, since it's gotta be believable.

Madisonville Pain Management Clinic

The metal-flake-brown Silverado sits beneath a Madisonville poplar tree dropping its leaves onto South College Street, just down from Leeza's operation, though they never see her enter or exit.

"She finally got smart on the waiting time," said Ed, looking at the old yellow brick building, a duplex with identical storefronts and matching second-story apartments.

The previous week, the customer line entering the clinic wrapped all around the building and down the street, embarrassing Sarge, who thought more of Leeza's skills. He'd guessed that only 20% of the Madisonville Clinic's pill seekers held legitimate prescriptions, and sponsors swamped the street unless the holding area soaked up the excess bodies.

"She fixed it, just like I predicted," he said.

Pain management customers idled in the large waiting room on rows of folding chairs in the south apartment, getting up to walk down the stairs when their names were called, one-at-a-time, stepping briefly onto the street, and then sliding into the north store—the actual clinic. There they slapped down their $350 cash with the secretary, and received their brain-numbing bounty after a five-minute chat with physician assistant Sandra Fogle.

Ed and Sarge watched Jesse Davis step onto the street from the waiting-room side of the duplex, look both ways, and enter the pain clinic. They eyed him sadly shaking his head. Jesse's brother, Fred, was Buddy McCoy's Chief Deputy, right-hand man, and head-knocker.

When Jesse stumbled out of the Madisonville Pain Management Clinic ten minutes after walking in, they waved him over.

"You guys are pretty obvious, sitting out here," said Jesse.

"And for a guy who's never worked a day in his life, never picked up a heavy object, or broke a sweat outside of playing strip poker with a hooker, you look *somewhat* out-of-place walking away from a pain management clinic," said Sarge.

"Born with scoliosis," said Jesse.

"Bullshit," said Ed. "There's nothing genetically wrong with your spine. Smoking dope for thirty-some years, eating like a pig, never taking a day of exercise, and sitting on that piss-poor excuse for furniture is what messed up your back."

"Small towns suck," Jesse philosophized. "Everybody knows your business."

"And when we don't, we just make something up," said Ed with a smile.

"How much does Leeza give you up front to drive over here and grab a bottle of oxycodone?" asked Sarge.

"Leeza's off stage, and you know it," said Jesse. "Pussycat handles oxy."

"Because he doesn't eat opiates," said Ed. "Do any Wrucks eat pills?"

"Bushrod Stout," said Jesse. "But he's the muscle. And never gets high on the job, best I can tell."

"Slowburn's a grass burner. Pussy's a juicer. Bushrod eats an oxy now and then. Leeza's straight, unless you count Irish whiskey and Salems. What about the kids?" asked Ed.

"He'll burn a little weed, sip a little beer after a win at the track, but he's looking ahead to a career outside the pill mills," said Jesse.

"If they continue with success, he'll have money to accomplish whatever he puts his mind to," noted Ed. "What about Sunny?"

"Sunny's Lucinda's opiate peddler. Leeza manages Madisonville, Lucinda Kituwah Falls. And Sunny's freakin' crazy; Bo's opposite. It's amazing they're twins," said Jesse. "Sunny thinks he's ten-foot-tall and bulletproof. Nothing's going to change that until he learns otherwise."

"He got a wake-up call the other day," said Sarge.

"I heard the judge dismissed the attempted rape charge," said Jesse.

Sarge looked down and kicked at the curb.

"Sunny's whacked when he's working?" asked Ed.

"The reason the Wrucks are so successful is that they're stone-cold business people. They let off steam on the weekends, but Sunny can't handle drugs, and they don't let him use during the week. He's the wildcard, and if they didn't keep an eye on him, the whole ball of wax might melt. But they let him go on the weekends to keep him happy."

"Binger," concluded Ed.

"'Zactly," confirmed Jesse.

"Just a matter of time before he goes off the rails," said Sarge.

"I reckon," said Jesse, slipping the proffered Franklin into his T-shirt pocket.

"Aren't you afraid of Leeza?" asked Ed.

"Hell, yes," said Jesse, looking up and down the street before striding toward the alley.

Sarge looked back at the clinic window and noticed Fogle staring right at him and Ed. She quickly turned away and vanished.

Sarge Walker's Farm House

Sam finished her history lesson, a recent newspaper article on the number of times Afghanistan changed hands, only to remain a tribal cat box, a sandy border between two continents, unfazed by invasion.

Imagine that, she thought to herself.

Sarge slipped in the back door and sat across the large, round oak dining table, then stared at the pheasant pictured on the placemat.

"What?" asked Sam.

Sarge stared.

"Where have you been hanging out the last few days?" she asked.

"Ed and I surveilled the pain management clinics in Madisonville and Kituwah Falls," he finally said.

"Why?"

"We think they're in the hands of folks who've moved up here from Florida."

"Most folks with a working brain already know something's wrong when a third of the population's stumbling around on painkillers, driving cars into the side of buildings, leaving food burning on the stove, and forgetting to change diapers on their kids until their little legs are black."

"We're figuring out their system," said Sarge.

"For a bust?" asked Sam.

Sarge sat looking at the placemat. "The woman managing the Madisonville clinic," he began.

"Leeza Wruck," said Sam. "Drives around in a black Cadillac SUV with Lucinda Hornback. The woman who manages Kituwah Falls PMC. Everybody already knows it."

Sarge squared in the chair, turned to Sam, squeezed her left shoulder and said, "Leeza Wruck is your biological mother."

***

Jasper peddled his bicycle the blacktop half-mile to Sam's in pine-scented, yellow half-moonlight, wondering about the future.

Part of him knew they should attend separate universities, date other people, find themselves—as if they were lost—and then get back together, which would prove beyond doubt that it was meant to be.

His parents met at the University of Tennessee, where his dad majored in electrical engineering and his mother did elementary education.

Hailing from San Antonio, his mother Alice had fallen in love with pictures of the lush mountains within the Great Smoky Mountains National Park when she first began to read. She applied to the University of Tennessee after high school, and her parents granted her wish to seek an out-of-state education. Their ancestors were Tennesseans, after all.

The moniker *Volunteers* derived from the Mexican War, where willing participants won land grants if they survived the fracas in Texas. Tennesseans applied by the droves, not necessarily out of love of country or dedication to the cause.

Volunteers, indeed.

Alice Thompson met Cornelius Whitlock walking down Knoxville's Cumberland Avenue during their sophomore fall semester. Cornelius stood looking into the large window of a sporting goods store, and Alice studied his reflection: tall, thin. A long-distance runner, Cornelius loved fast water, as well, especially fishing the falling streams winding their way through the Nantahala Gorge. He peered at the small crafts hanging from the shop's ceiling. After he strode inside to gasp at their price tags, he noticed Alice standing at his shoulder.

Which led to a discussion about kayaks.

Which led to a date.

Which led to romance, marriage, and Jasper.

Alice hired into the Monroe County School System upon her graduation, and Cornelius signed up with the TVA. Following a quick Texas marriage and honeymoon, they bought an old Cape Cod outside Kituwah Falls and enjoyed five years of bliss before Jasper arrived.

And happiness waxed.

Until Alice drowned saving a life swirling down the tempestuous Nantahala.

Jasper and Cornelius flew to San Antonio to visit Alice's parents two years after her funeral. After two days walking around the city, they drove west out past Hondo, turning home west of D'Harris.

Struck by the vastness of prairie, Jasper bounced in the back seat of his grandfather's Pontiac, remembering the soft embrace of the Appalachians left behind.

The natural beauty around Kituwah Falls had never pierced his consciousness until he experienced flat brown fields rolling on toward eternity.

They stopped at a wayside picnic area, a small table surrounded by brown cedars beside the road, and Jasper sat with his arms wrapped around himself, bent into the wind, eyes slatted against the driving wind, piercing sand particles into his flesh.

His eyes teared at such loneliness on the plains, only the howling wind and whatever thread of material you carried for clothes keeping you company. The thought of spending the night out there, against the elements, evoked a shudder.

The East was full of water and fuel and food and people, mountains with wrapping arms, comforting, keeping the past close, the sound of ancestors echoing in waterfalls. At that moment, Jasper realized he'd live out the rest of his life in Kituwah Falls, though he'd make a point of traveling the world to appreciate the Cherokee National Forest even more, and to learn.

As a child, Jasper believed that life was simple. Hating change, he put his faith in family, God, nature, and that family down the road, the Walkers.

But when his mom lost her life enjoying the thing she loved, life's complexity crashed around his ears in mournful epiphany.

The Little Prince spoke to him in the darkness of his thoughts: *The stars are very beautiful because of a flower that cannot be seen.*

Things would never be simple again.

And so it was with Samantha, and their relationship. During their first 15 years together, she held no physical attraction whatsoever. Like a sister, more than anything.

And since they'd grown up swapping snot under the kitchen table, beneath the outstretched legs of their coffee-drinking, jaw-jacking parents always discussing the latest project, national politics, trout season, history, deer hunting, river levels for kayaking, needs of the local church, the latest missionary trip rebuilding homes in the dark hollows of impoverished Appalachia, the importance of literacy to the Eastern Band of the Cherokee—so many issues, so little time, the gift of ambition running through both of them, and the complexity of knowing each other too-well, too-soon.

Then Sam turned 17. And budded out. Full bloom.

Argh.

Jasper smiled to himself and thought:

If it weren't for that rabbit, I'd be a daddy right now.

Skidding up to Sam's door, he leaned the bike on the front porch and knuckled the door. Instead of Sam stepping into his arms, Sarge walked out with a dour look on his face and led Jasper down to the creek where they walked in the moonlight, listening to the wind toss the branches, and Jasper became enlightened about the Wrucks and their soon-to-be-dissolved opiate empire.

Rosie's Steak and Seafood Restaurant, Knoxville

Odessa Blankenship called a celebratory dinner for Friday evening after the post-tax financial report indicated record-breaking profits for the Madisonville and Kituwah Falls Pain Management Clinics.

Above-board, legitimate customer profits for each clinic netted nearly $650,000 taxable for 2015. The under-the-table net averaged $1.5 million per clinic, a figure Odessa neglected to share, though she realized Leeza and Lucinda could easily calculate ballpark figures via simple logic and the percentage they received in their own pay.

Leeza, Lucinda, Sandra, Kristen Burley, Odessa, and her beau Ron shared a table at the back of the steak-and-seafood restaurant off I-40, next to the Turkey Creek Mall in West Knoxville, minutes from Ron and Odessa's toney abode fronting Fort Louden Lake.

Odessa threw big parties on a quarterly basis, rewarding her clinics' staff with holiday-themed food and professional entertainment. But after a brief appearance ending with a rah-rah speech, she quietly retreated while the semi-raucous crowd partied into the wee hours, carefully, stifling exuberance so sleeping neighbors remained undisturbed.

Odessa raised her wine glass in a toast, everyone mirroring the gesture, and she spoke loudly over the low-but-constant restaurant din: "To pain alleviation!"

"To pain alleviation!" came the echo.

Busboys began clearing dessert plates as Ron called for the check, when a smiling, horse-toothed, red-haired man in his mid-forties approached and tapped Lucinda on the left shoulder.

"Harry Weems!" squealed Lucinda as she rose to embrace him, bumping the table with her large thighs as she stood, jangling silverware and overturning Odessa's coffee cup, which splashed brown liquid onto the white table linen.

Leeza's upper lip curved into a snarl as Lucinda stage-whispered into Harry's ear, then Lucinda slapped him loudly on the butt before he ran off, following Lucinda's order to vamoose.

"And who might that be?" asked Odessa, exchanging a curious, furrowed-brow glance with Leeza as Lucinda plopped back down, drinking off her remaining beer in a single gulp.

"Guy's name is Harry Weems," said Lucinda. "He's a medical equipment salesman I met last week when we called on the Kituwah clinic. He's full of great ideas."

"And what were you doing showing your face down at the clinic?" asked Odessa, blood darkening around the edges of her painted face.

"Oh, just making sure things were in good running order," said Lucinda.

After a pregnant pause, Odessa turned to square her shoulders in Lucinda's direction, and enunciated slowly in cool tones: "That's Kristen's job."

"Oh, yeah?" said Lucinda, blood rising to her cheeks. Her right hand shook perceptively, whirlpooling the remaining foam.

Leeza kicked Lucinda's foot under the table, and their eyes locked. "Yes, Lucinda," said Leeza. "Kristen performs the day-to-day. You agreed to oversee the operation and all its sponsors from *outside* the premises. No need to draw attention to yourself. That's foolish. Everyone in Kituwah Falls knows you're not seeking pain medication, so what would you be doing inside?"

Lucinda dropped the beer glass, pulled her bottom lip under her front teeth, bit down in a way that hardened her eyes, and retained a strangled speechlessness.

The moment passed.

Ron signed for the check, and the startled group arose in toto to begin a tipsy retreat to their cars and the headlight-illuminated-trek home.

Leeza remained at the table with Odessa and Ron for five minutes before joining Lucinda, who was crying on her cell phone in the Escalade's shotgun seat.

Samantha Walker's Journal

They say Jesus was out in the desert for 40 days, talking to God, bantering with the devil. Jesus was out there listening to the Evil One's grandiose promises of earthly pleasure and treasure, but ultimately taking the high road instead, the alternate path.

The road less traveled, Mr. Frost.

But it only took three days for me in the woods; 72 hours of solitary confinement in the Cherokee National Forest, listening to the creaking and chirping and howling and babbling and sighing and soughing of the other billion-plus inmates, animal, vegetable, mineral, macro, micro, wind, earth, fire, and the spirit between.

Now that I'm out of the woods, I'll say that it's a difficult task loving your enemies.

Loving and *Sunny Wruck* struggle to fit together inside a sentence. But if you pull off the cosmic trick of loving your enemy, benefits include:

1) Freaking them out;
2) Making them paranoid;
3) Exposing their evil to the world.

Loving deadheads turns the tables, tosses the ball of negativity into their court. So I'm not going to burn their place down just yet. I'll love them instead, though arson holds sweet instant gratification.

Believe me, I was super-pissed going into the forest, realizing the county-killing Wrucks are blood kin. Well, one of them. I'd never be able to swallow blood kinship with Sunny Boy, or his half-decent-brother Bo, who's trying unsuccessfully to hide that spark of goodness inside.

Bo being the smasher of my collarbone, nonetheless.

Jesus tells us there's basically two things we need to consider; the rest of it, all the conniving and rule-making and rule-breaking in the *Old Testament*, and all the parables in the *New Testament*, actually fall under two commands.

Pastor Clawson at the First Presbyterian says we should "take all them *schisms* and *isms* and throw 'em out the winder! They's the cause of all the bickerin' and infightin' this here world's ever saw!"

You have to keep clear of the front row some Sunday mornings, because he'll Gallagher his spittle all over you.

"Stick to them two simple commands," he says, "and you'll be all right."

One: Love God.

We learned in Sunday school that back in the *Old Testament* days, the Jewish chief priest would symbolically lay the sins of the people on this little hapless, unknowing sacrificial goat... sending it out into the wilderness to be gobbled up by wolves.

Some folks blame God for death, disease, war, bad mortgages, early pregnancies, idiotic politicians, pimples, diaper rash, bedsores, homelessness, bedbugs, blah blah blah. He's a handy scapegoat, indeed. Even better than Jews or Muslims. Women. Homosexuals. Mexicans.

The Big Guy is invisible, so you don't have to build ovens to burn Him up, devise bombs to drop on His head, fashion guns to shoot Him, weave rope to hang Him from a handy dogwood while peering through those uneven holes in your itchy homemade Klan-smock.

No work involved, outside of keeping fiery furnaces of hate stoked-and-coaled.

For me, He's positive and omnipresent. Flashing Jasper's mischievous smile. Calming through Sarge's patience. Shimmering in the far blue mountains running endlessly east and south off the Cherohala. Scenting the cinnamon-ish Carolina rhododendron. Providing the creamy citrus rush of springtime Fraser Magnolia as I throttle-up Ole Blue through ancient forests that stand beside clear rushing streams, with the heroic legacy of JT Walker running through my veins. The glint in a happy mutt's eyes. Einstein's theories. The Big Bang proving that only a higher power in a separate dimension could survive the blast. I could recite His power for days, and drain the ink from a dozen pens, and I'd just begin to list the nature of His intent. He's everywhere at once, in my corner, and I realize that the closer our relationship—the harder I work to hold up my end of the bargain—the easier it will be to deal with all that lies ahead.

But maintaining that is up to me.

Problems aren't going to evaporate if you love Him; they aren't dissolving for me—that's for sure. He'll never sugarcoat or dismiss them. He provides a short respite, the shade of a dappled bush in the desert. Just enough shade, just enough thirst-killing water, a listening ear, and then you can stumble forward. With life.

When Jasper and I decided to wait a while to consummate our relationship, that didn't make us less horny. Ah! But leaning on the Big Guy instead, knowing it's the right-thing-to-do, makes the situation tolerable.

Barely.

But do-able.

If we were living in Leeza Wruck's environment, we'd probably have our own prostitution ring up and running by now, subjugating pill sponsors needing an extra $50 a week. Bend over, sit on that, there you go, here's your $50. When you rash up and dry out, we'll toss you away and call in another warm body. There's a waiting room full of Jonesing pill poppers waiting for magic pills.

Hear how nasty I can be if I let go? Nastiness runs off of me whenever I think of what's coming next, what we're going to have to do to combat all these changes, confront these people, drive them off.

And that's why I can't juice. It may be that little bit of Cherokee blood, or that whole bunch of Irish, but on the second drink, I blab exactly what I'm thinking. And it goes downhill from there.

The bottom line: each of us has the ability to look at a situation, consider the options, and make positive choices that ultimately make life easier—by foregoing instant gratification—and forward life goals.

Or not. We won't make the right choices every time, but if we're thinking ahead, we can show the Big Guy we're trying. Grace will cover the failures, if our hearts are pure.

Kituwah Falls—and every other town in America—is loaded with stories about large, dysfunctional families simultaneously churning out saints and hellraisers, doctors and doodle heads, priests and purse snatchers, crooked police and honest thieves, celibate lunatics and lusty preachers. The entire gamut of bruised apples, often polar opposites, falling off the same family tree.

So the way of the universe *must* go beyond genetics. And environment. Because all these different personalities and outcomes derived from the same house and the same genes, the same experiences unfolding with infinite variety.

Well, they all had the same mother, anyway.

You can always tell who your mother is. Unfortunately.

Maybe that's why parts of *The Bible* trace family trees using the mothers as benchmarks. Finding your biological dad might be more difficult.

Which is the irony of my situation.

And perhaps the key to the puzzle of life is simply choice, the eternally looping tale of Adam and Eve. Jezebel and Ahab.

Bo makes bad choices. His *job* is bill-collecting for Lucinda, and since he threatens—and sometimes carries out, I'm told—violence on the indebted, he's definitely no prince. But there's something there that could blossom, given the chance. That's my intuition.

And another bizarre life-fact is that there really aren't many tried and true bad guys in the world.

Movies, TV, most books and short stories often depend on these one-dimensional characters, cardboard-cutouts splashed black or white.

That's unrealistic.

The truth is, each of us is the lead actor in the mega-blockbuster running inside our little heads. No one acknowledges the bad guy in that gray-gooey-space between his-or-her ears; no one sees a bad guy gazing back from the mirror.

When I witness someone at school being stupid or mean, I try to consider what caused that behavior.

One day, Billy Smithpeters—who everyone knows has some issues, mostly developmental—he's gotta great heart, all the girls love him, as he's harmless, smiles all the time. Well, Billy stood in the gym with all of us, waiting for the first bell, just hanging out, talking to his sister Lily. Football jock Jake Malone starts mocking Billy. Walks and talks and smiles and shakes his arms up and down like Billy, kind of a nervous tic thing, only Jake meant to make him look stupid.

Billy likes girls, so you know Jake's bullying was killing him. Then Jake gets in Billy's face and jerks his shoulders back-and-forth. Billy turns beet red; he's so embarrassed.

Jasper sat beside me, watching the whole thing, ten rows up in the middle of the bleachers, going over our physics homework.

Whoosh! Jasper leaps off the tenth row, flies over the heads of a half-dozen kids, smashing down on top of Jake.

They both pop right up following impact, and Jasper immediately slips around and wrestles Jake into a reverse-hammerlock, taking the big football tackle to the ground screaming. Really puts the squash on him, and soon Jake cries and whines like a fifth-grade bully. Separates Jake's shoulder where Jasper landed on him.

The principal sorts it all out and makes Jasper clean the boys' toilets for a month.

So back to my point. Why would Jake pick on Billy? What's to gain?

Jake's one of the good guys. Comes from a decent family—genetics should have worked in his favor—he has everything he needs, has tons of friends, even a girlfriend. So what's the deal?

Apparently, Jake found out that none of his athletic scholarships came through, none of the local colleges signed him to play, due to his academic record. His grades suck so much, he can't get into a decent college, so it looks like he's stuck in Kituwah Falls, carrying bags and waiting on farmers at the feed store.

Smiling Billy set him off. Maybe it was Billy's situation, not having a care in the world.

I'm glad Jasper kicked Jake's tail, but sad that Jake morphed into a jerk-stick over his failed dreams. Like it was Billy's fault Jake forgot to study.

Too many kids think they're going to be sports stars, despite the fact that odds of winning the lottery are much better than suiting up next to LeBron.

Ain't gonna happen.

Mr. Stephens says some jocks slip over to the technical track and do well, becoming electricians and HVAC technicians and builders and 3-D print masters, diesel mechanics and computer gurus, but they get a late start. I'm not saying they're dumb, just coddled.

But now, you understand why I question the solid-black *bad guy* stereotype versus the solid-white *good guy* cowboy-hat-division-of-right-and-wrong.

Ain't no such thing.

Had that rabbit not mysteriously appeared at the window, I'd be ready to pop right now, yellow and green baby poop stench soon filling the air. Folks would say I wasn't Christian dropping a kid into the world out of wedlock. They'd also spit on me if I aborted the child.

Amanda's cousin at another high school—her parents, when they found out she was pregnant, forced her to undergo an abortion to keep the family name clean. She wanted the baby. But her parents drove her to Chattanooga, far enough away so they'd probably not run into anyone they knew, waited in the car during the procedure, and then practically disowned her when she came back crying. Loving, *Christian* parents.

When was the last time you saw a Bible-thumper adopt a crack baby? An alcohol fetal syndrome baby? An opiate baby? I don't see many adopting *healthy* babies around here. Sure, rich couples in big cities scour the Earth to locate and adopt healthy babies. But in the middle of the Bible Belt?

Not so much.

I'm sure it happens. This is a big, diverse country with lots of wonderful folks in it. But I don't see any *locals* adopting a problem baby. God never tells them to do that.

I've asked, "Why don't you adopt a fetal alcohol baby? You're against abortion, aren't you?"

They get this quizzical look on their face, and then a light bulb flashes in their brains, and they invariably say, "God didn't lay that on my heart right now."

How convenient.

Maniac Bible-thumpers blow up abortion clinics, kill and maim innocent people, but they somehow fail to adopt special-needs babies who really need loving parents.

That would be *work*. That would be *risky*; would take *courage* and *faith*. Those first steps out of the boat and onto the waves.

The work of Jesus. Mother Theresa.

Folks aren't willing to dig that deep and put their money where their cruel mouths twitch.

Gandhi once said, "I like your Christ. I do not like your Christians. Your Christians are so unlike your Christ."

Ouch.

Terrible feelings, Mr. Stephens. Thank God all this is hidden in a journal, invisible to the sheet-wearers who punch uneven holes in their pillowcases.

Jasper and I both felt blue when the rabbit stared us down. Sex rocks! I know that in my bones, though I can only imagine. Well, we fool around a little. Just being around Jasper tweaks my tension.

I'm turning inside out, and Jasper complains he sticks to his bed three-days-a-week from wet dreams, says he needs a giant spatula to pry himself off the mattress when he wakes and smells the kitchen coffee brewing.

Choices.

So, loving God and mistrusting Bible-thumpers and snake-oil-salesmen comes natural. Bigly!

Since the Wrucks moved to town two years ago, parading down main street in their fleet of pill-bought-late-model-vehicles, the Madisonville and Kituwah Falls Pain Management Clinics popped up like poisonous mushrooms, and now zombies stumble down the streets, needing *brains* in the form of pills and powders.

Four deaths so far throughout Monroe County, though no officials examine the cases, except the coroner and the pathologist performing autopsies.

Ed and Sarge spoke to fatality-stricken-families, and each acknowledged the victims used painkillers, received opiates from the clinics, and two overdose victims mixed pills with alcohol. One fell down the stairs, breaking her neck, and one's daddy backed up the family car and squashed her in the driveway.

We've known most of these folks our whole lives: Dylan Dykes. Sidney Hollyfield. Glenda-Jane Jackson. Ashley Sizer.

Sean's old man, Ted, high on Vicodin, crunched Ashley's bones with the Plymouth. His three-year-old daughter!

Two: Love Your Neighbor.

There's the problem, at least for this girl. The *rub*. So many *homo sapiens* are unlovable.

Jasper is totally loveable, but there are days when I'd bum-rush him off the edge of the Grand Canyon, he makes me so angry. When you know someone well, you push their buttons. We push each other's buttons.

That's the way of the world, I reckon.

And when Sarge sat down, took my hand, and announced that Leeza Wruck's my biological mother, well. Number Two carries a double meaning, indeed.

Love your neighbor as you love yourself. Love your enemy.

Ahahahahahahahahaha!

So I sat in the woods, where thinking runs deep, rain drizzling down, then slacking off and turning to frost in the wee hours, deer stepping out to graze under the half-moon, a buck snorting in the meadow, nighthawks rushing through the air, a raccoon wobbling down to the river for a meal of mussels… The comforting sounds, the deep-woods smell, rotting leaves, loam and pine, the comforts of my backyard— the Cherokee National Forest—and I considered the words, the information, the genetic link, the blood in my veins, and what to do about it.

Part of me wants to sneak over to the Wrucks' late Saturday night—early Sunday morning—after they'd drunk their whiskey, eaten their pills, smoked their weed, gobbled their greasy burgers, and headed to their unkempt beds unaware, so I could sneak in, splash a five-gallon can of gasoline-mixed-with-diesel-fuel around the house and garage. Gas mixed with diesel won't explode, but ignites quickly and continues to burn. Every camp-fire-freak knows gasoline alone explodes. Oh, baby, make it ¾ diesel and the starter lives another day. Splash that concoction all around, and be done with the whole stinking mess in one night. They'd all, though maybe not Bo, be passed out dead-to-the-world on Sunday morning.

Dead to the world!

They certainly wouldn't be rising early to worship the Lord, after all.

Watching that whole operation melt down into a black hunk of tar in my mind's eye made me smile, for sure.

Miss Christian! Love your neighbor as you would love yourself. Love your enemy. Turn the other cheek.

Command Two is a nut to swaller.

But here's my prayer for the Wrucks, and I don't care if you listen in, Mr. Stephens.

Dear Lord:

Please help these people realize the curse they have laid upon the people of Kituwah Falls. Please open the eyes of these death merchants to the consequences of their actions, and help them to realize their current path will end in destruction, as surely as their actions are an affront to humanity, and to You, as well. Amen.

Do I think this prayer will work?

That depends on the Wrucks more than God. Because they already know their business killed four Monroe Countians, and they *knew* three-year-old Ashley Sizer.

Sean and Sunny are best buds, after all.

And maybe it's up to the Walkers and Whitlocks to remind the Wrucks about the concept of choice.

After three days contemplating the options, I've narrowed the action plan down to four possibilities:

1) Go to war unannounced and take them down in a surprise assault;

2) Call the FBI and let the Feds handle it;

3) Wait and surveil for more information;

4) Call them out, make them realize the destruction headed their way, and ask them to move on before the hammer comes down.

I decided number three is the easiest, but Sarge and Ed already know Leeza's in charge of Madisonville. Lucinda's managing Kituwah Falls. Each has a physician-of-record to legally obtain the drugs, physician assistants at each clinic for medical supervision-recruitment-retention-expansion, and each clinic has sponsors and debt collectors, known to the citizens of both towns.

Ed and Sarge gained intel on the Knoxville chief. This whole ring moved up from Tampa when the heat drove them north. Five-Oh heat, not ambient temperature heat.

Which means Sarge already engaged choice two, or will shortly.

So number four, that's my plan of action, confronting the Wrucks with words, not gasoline, diesel, shotguns, rifles, or crossbow bolts. Not yet.

But I'll have to ask Sarge first. They may not blow the head off a teenage girl right away, which would give me time to talk them into heading down the highway.

All this is between the journal and me, Mr. Stephens. Student-teacher privilege, sir.

Blankenship-Williams Residence, Knoxville

"When did she tell you she was leaving?" asked Odessa.

"Never did," said Leeza. "Just stopped calling last week, and I haven't seen her in person since the party at the steakhouse."

"Do you have anyone on the inside of her new business?" asked Odessa.

"Just Wayne Fogle. That Weems creep hired all new people, mostly fresh graduates from nursing schools and newly-minted physician assistants."

"Where did he get the money to set up shop?" asked Odessa.

"I have no idea," said Leeza. "But he did sign on two of your people up the food chain to make it work."

Odessa just looked at Leeza, blood rising up her face like a rash creeping on slow-motion film. "Not the judges."

Leeza simply nodded with her head bowed.

Odessa rose quietly, stood thinking for a full minute, then picked up her iced tea glass, turned, and hurled it into the screen of the 65-inch Samsung flatscreen TV at the end of the living room.

Buladeen yelped in surprise from the bedroom door.

Ron, hearing the crash, emerged from his basement man-cave and listened carefully as Odessa outlined the rebellion—and intended response—with a shaking voice.

Sweetwater Pain Management Clinic

Lucinda and Wayne sat across from each other in the conference room at the back of the clinic, door closed, muffled sounds of the busy office lightly penetrating the barrier.

"You promised Leeza you would rejoin your sponsorship at Kituwah Falls," she reminded him.

"I did," said Wayne.

"How's that working out with Sandra?" asked Lucinda.

Wayne looked off at the wall, his features tightening.

"We'll make it work, for now," he said, turning back to face Lucinda.

"Bushrod will mess you up if he thinks you're double-dipping over here."

"I reckon. But he doesn't frequent Knoxville, and my clients are from the far east side, mostly Blaine and Rutledge, off the pike. Who's running the show in Kituwah, now that you pulled out?"

"Leeza's handling both clinics. Until she can find a suitable replacement."

"Who's the strong-arm over here?"

"One of Harry's old softball buddies," she said. "Randy Plunkett."

"Jubal Plunkett's kid, the old tight-end?"

"Yep."

"But Judge Plunkett's in Odessa's pocket."

Lucinda cackled. "Fits in lotsa pockets. As long as pills and cash flow his way."

Marvin Hughes's Residence

Bushrod Stout, head of collections for the Madisonville Pain Management Clinic, under the direction of Leeza Wruck, sat in his fully-tricked-out silver 2015 Ford Explorer Platinum Edition. The Exploder, Bushrod called it, a nod to the days when rear-end collisions trapped hapless victims inside, engulfed in flames. He lifted a fine set of binoculars, Celestron Skymasters, and glassed the rickety front porch nailed haphazardly to Marvin Hughes's single-wide, six miles southwest of Kituwah Falls, off the Mecca Pike.

A pack of well-fed Rottweilers lazed about the yard under the shade of various trees and vehicles, waiting to sound alarm should an interloper cross into their territory. Bushrod used to visit his old friend Marvin before he started breeding and selling the large canines, but the first time one of the beasts snuck up behind Stout and bit his ass, he left Marvin alone. A natural sneak, Bushrod held other snakes in high contempt.

Drug sellers often used Pitbulls and Rottweilers as early-warning devices, noted Bushrod, thinking that a pack of agitated Rottweilers gave Marvin time to prepare for an intrusion.

Marvin finally wandered out of the loose-hanging aluminum door at half-past-noon, taking a minute to stretch, yawn, and squint his bloodshot eyes at the midday sun.

After facing south, bending over slowly, and reaching into the mailbox—probably expecting to find April's SSI check—a .17 caliber Hornaday-Hornet-varmint-round entered his right buttock, passed through both fat slabs of gluteus maximus, sailed through the open door, and lodged in the refrigerator after passing through the orange forehead of a Donald Trump campaign poster.

One week later, a sizable cash payment arrived inside a wrinkled-but-insured yellow package, hand-delivered by a USPS carrier to the motorcycle shop behind Leeza Wruck's new brick ranch off Unicoi Church Road.

Bo Wruck's Journal

Well, I am certainly spilling my guts all over this journal.

You're going to burn it when I'm through with probation, I know, but it's in my school backpack all evening, and through the day, until I turn it in to you on Friday afternoon. Maybe I should hide it where no one here would ever look, like inside the oven, inside the washing machine, or inside Leeza's family Bible. Can't believe they even have one, with Digger Byrum soaking Cocke County in moonshine all those years. I did sneak a peek once, and just inside the cover is a family tree originating with Patrick Byrum, a Revolutionary War soldier.

Leeza loves watching me race. You can see her jumping up and down on the sidelines when I make a pass. Not exactly warm and fuzzy around me and Sunny, but she ain't cold, either. Distracted. Hardly ever in the moment.

Me, I'm like an animal when it comes to living-in-the-moment. Full concentration on whatever I'm doing, most days. That's a gift when it comes to motocross. Maybe life in general.

Leeza can't cook, doesn't clean much, and I expect she'll have another house built when this one's trashed beyond recognition. She's a big drinker and smoker, but for some reason, she's real kind to animals, though she doesn't keep any, since we're always running the roads, and the three Junk Yard Dawgs are animal enough. Would probably eat out of a bowl if you set it down on the floor in front of them.

She actually likes Sunny and me. I can tell by the way she praises us when I win a race, or when Sunny brings home an extra wad of cash.

He's a good pistol shot, too. Him and Sean practice all the time up at the old abandoned dump. They used to shoot rats, but they're all shot up now, the survivors moved to town where there's more trash to eat. White trash equals lots of leftover pizza crust.

Sunny carries this little bitty pistol that fits neat in his pants. You wouldn't even know it was there. But it'll fool you. Smith & Wesson 442 hammerless .38 Special Airweight. He can knock the eye out of a squirrel at ten yards; pretty good for a light pistol. He and Sean always practice when they're not dealing. Don't spend any time on schoolwork, that's for sure.

I'm in the woods riding the motorcycle, and he's plinking cans with a .38 Special.

He doesn't carry in school, Mr. Stephens. After all these public school shootings, he knows they'll hammer him if he's caught. He won't risk jail time that would make him dependent on a shiny-chrome walker when he gets out. Nope. He keeps it in his Jeep, or his street bike, when he's not in school.

You ever hear how Sunny got his nickname? Bet not. He'd bust my ass if he knew I wrote it down on paper, even if it was for your eyes only. He don't like you much. He thinks he knows it all, and teachers generally piss him off.

When we was just ten year-old kids, we was in East Tampa, in the middle of a trailer park. EZ-Dayz Trailer Park, it was called. You ain't never seen trailer parks until you visit East Tampa. Looked like the whole world lived in a trailer park. EZ-Dayz was where Leeza made her first fortune in opiates. We tried to live low, but it was obvious other kids lived hand-to-mouth, eating paint chips off porch posts and such. Parents all strung out on pills, weed, meth, you name it. EZ-Dayz. Leeza fed a lot of kids, I'll give her that. Frozen pizza microwaved. Can't say that it was nutritious, but she did nuke it up, plus hand out bags of tater chips they could stick in their mouths. She makes some of these people here take payment in groceries or she won't deal with them.

Anyway, this is the story, often told by Slowburn when Sunny's not around.

Slowburn was sitting in the side yard with us ten year-olds, and we're jumping in and out of one of them plastic pools you blow up, the kind that makes Slowburn red in the face and wheezing from burning plant material down in them lungs, you know. All of a sudden Mason—Sunny's real name—decides he's going to stare down the sun.

"Don't do that," says Slowburn.

"Why not?" asks Mason.

"It'll burn your eyes," says Slowburn.

You could see the anger rising up my brother's face, and that bottom lip starts twitching.

If you ever see that, Mr. Stephens, it's a sure sign that you better get moving in the other direction as quick as possible, because .38 Special slugs are easier to take in the back and butt than they are in the face and guts.

Mason intentionally sets his hands on his hips, flings his head back, and stares down the sun.

Slowburn figures the sun will take care of the problem all by itself.

Nope. Mason just stares and stares and stares down that Florida sun until Slowburn freaks out, starts thinking about what it would be to look after a blind child, and has to knock Mason on the side of the head, which makes him go berserk. Slowburn has to tie him up in a kitchen chair in the trailer for the rest of the morning.

When Mason finally calms down, Slowburn drives us to the nearest clinic, and the doc there says he'd suffered *solar retinopathy*, which happens when too much ultraviolet light floods the retina. Supposed to be extremely painful, but Mason just stuck out that lower lip and winced.

He finally recovers a week later, but then he says he has these yellow spots in the center of his eyes when he's looking off into the distance.

Sunny Boy. That's what we all call him now, after that EZ-Dayz stare down.

Now I know you're a man driven by logic, Mr. Stephens. I know what you're thinking. How can a kid with yellow spots in his eyes be a crack pistol shot?

Simple. He carries the Airweight in his pants waist above his right pocket, crosses over, draws with his dominant right hand, and sights through his dominant right eye. And he swears that yellow spot lines directly up with the target. Built-in laser sights! Burnt-in forever by an act of stubbornness, defying the sun, of all things. What a kid. My fraternal twin, but he feels like a yin to my opposing yang.

I got off on this tangent, up this bunny trail, but food is the issue.

Pizza.

That's what we eat, most days. There's a big stack of them in the white 20 cubic-foot freezer in the middle of our big, beautiful, new porch house built by some fancy contractor out of Knoxville.

Slowburn tried to reason with Leeza before that contractor's men swarmed in and tore up the ground and slung cement, then started machine-gunning nails into boards, Mexicans running around in the sun like ants on a giant anthill. If them Mexicans ever get organized, the lazy white trash will be in deep trouble, Mr. Stephens. Guess they already are, or we wouldn't enjoy a booming pill business.

Not that pills only go down the dry mouths of poor white folks. Doctors, lawyers, Indian Chiefs, black professionals in Knoxville; all be sucking pills these days, let me tell you. I'm carrying the cash to prove it.

Anyway, Slowburn tried to tell her, "Driving that Cadillac battleship and building this big brick ranch is like advertising you're a drug dealer. Might as well put an ad on the evening news between the Depends and boner pill commercials."

"Bushrod drives the fanciest Ford Explorer you can buy!" she yelled back.

"Which proves he's an idiot," Slowburn returned.

Slowburn may *look* like a moron, he may *act* like a moron—he has tobacco spit in his beard and pizza droppings on his shirt; there's sweat stains under his arms, and yellow piss drippings on the top of his socks—but he does practice commonsense most days.

Leeza's not that dumb, usually, but I think she's sticking her neck out a little bit up here in Kituwah Falls, because she loves flaunting her success in the face of the local bluebloods. Maybe that's because she left here under a cloud all those years back.

She loves to burn Ed, Lois, Cornelius, and Sarge, too, but I consider them common folk from common stock—Indians and countrified Scots and Melungeons and such—even though they favor education, church, and manners. She knows it really irks them to see her rolling in the cash, maybe because they had to work hard for theirs. Or maybe there's another reason I'm not aware of. She's a mystery in ways, never revealing much about her past.

Nobody can tune a race bike like Cornelius. I'd trade him for Pussycat any day in the mechanic department. Nobody would ever catch me if old Corn was wrenching my Yamaha.

Not that Sam ain't talented. Never seen a girl hold a candle to her, motorcycle-wise. All the old-timer bikers here say her old man was special on the track, won the local championships hands down. She's got genetics.

Those advantages, plus Cornelius on the end of the screwdriver, make her tough to beat.

Which brings me back to the pizza.

I've got to find an edge if I want to win with consistency, and living on junk food is taking away my edge. If I have to nibble one more frozen cheese pizza, I'm going to kill somebody.

Cash ain't no problem, as you know. But we have to fend for ourselves when it comes to food, clothes, shoes, schoolbooks, etc.

Leeza's not sampling the product, so that's not the problem. Yeah, she sips Jameson in the evenings, and sucks Full-Flavor Kool-Filter Kings all day long.

But she doesn't eat pills. The smart ones in this racket never do.

Lucinda'll mix pills and booze and it's not a pretty thing to witness. You better be off the road when she comes swinging around a corner on your side of the yellow line.

Leeza ain't mean, but she hasn't the fabric to be a great mom, either. She's not technically our mom, anyway, and we've always looked out for ourselves. We'd grab pop tarts and nuke them. But this processed crap is holding me back on the racetrack. I just have to learn how to pick out good food and cook it, that's all. Can't be rocket surgery, as Sean says.

A man-boy my age shouldn't have a cooking responsibility hanging over him, but I can't win a 25 lap Moto on a frozen cheese pizza, a bag of beef jerky, or a chocolate bar washed down with three power drinks. Ain't happening. I could take the first Moto that way, maybe, but certainly not the third, and you have to take the final event to win.

You think you could show me the ropes, Mr. Stephens? Or maybe your wife? There's a kitchen in the Home Economics room. I wouldn't have to come over to your house or nothing.

But I can't take Home Ec. Sunny and Sean would laugh in my face.

Thanks for considering it, though, Mr. Stephens. I ain't begging. I can always figure it out on my own.

Samantha Walker's Journal

Had the strategy talk with Sarge over a week ago, and he wanted Jasper and me to chill and avoid the Wrucks. He knows it grieves us to see the townspeople affected, but he forbids us to act. I didn't know he and Ed already staked out the operation with a plan in mind.

Figures.

Sarge says he'll call a buddy of his in the TBI and unload all that he and Ed dug up, but they're trying to build a case right now, something that will stand. Since Sarge was first to arrive on the scene at the Sizers' driveway, he's grieving for this community more than we are, I guess, and I tend to follow his advice, even when I don't want to listen.

He did say we could get online at the library and research the opiate epidemic and the drug trade, however. In fact, he actually gave us an assignment: uncover how they make their business appear legitimate so that the cash keeps flowing. He told us about how they keep an extra room close to the PMCs, so there's no line of druggies wrapping around the block. He knows how their sponsorship system works, and that they use street-level pushers like Sunny and Pussycat to sell those pills that the sponsored drug seekers return to the gang after visiting the PMC. He knows Bo and Bushrod collect debts on those who don't return seed money, or when users renege on a deal.

So the key thing left to figure out is how they maintain legitimacy. All last week, while Ed and Sarge nailed down facts surrounding the big-honcho-pill-mill-boss in Knoxville, Jasper and I searched the internet through private chatrooms and open newspaper sources to uncover the Florida-Georgia opiate empire that moved up here in the last few years.

I scanned the Miami, Fort Myers, St. Petersburg, Tampa, and Jacksonville papers. Jasper went undercover and trolled the sleazy, drug-related chatrooms, because the library and school security software blocked us from the Dark-Side-Dark-Net, but Cornelius-the-Techie maintains a good connection at home, which is difficult on the edge of the Unicois, but the satellite feed worked during the clear weather last week. Jasper chatted with runny-mouth deadheads and scored information. I still want to pursue rural medicine, but sleuthing is a gas. Sarge thinks we'd make crack investigators, but it's really about using common sense and switching directions when leads deaden.

Florida cracked down on pill mills in the early part of the decade, and enforced strict regulations when national media picked up on their opiate death rate—eleven people a day at the height of their problem. *The Tampa Bay Times* ran an editorial after last Christmas that said those overdose death numbers went down on account of stronger enforcement of the rules related to the distribution of prescription pills. The state legislature wrote new laws in 2010 and 2011 that made life hard on the pill mills. They also came up with a program to closely watch drug prescriptions, track 'em, and mitigate doctor shopping. Most doctors were barred from giving out most narcotics in their clinics, and some couldn't prescribe hardcore narcotics at all anymore.

The bad guys simply drove north into unregulated pay dirt. Tennessee is finally catching up, but the Wrucks quickly adapted to changing circumstances. Wouldn't be surprised if they pulled up stakes and headed to West Virginia if Tennessee ever gets its act together. That's their pattern.

We struck gold with Chattanooga and North Georgia papers, when I discovered a pill mill editorial about Dalton—right across the state line from Chattanooga—which described pill-mill-suspects spilling the beans for reduced jail time. Police suspected these low-level-operators feared retribution from higher-food-chain mobsters, and sought a government witness-protection program.

The Dalton Daily Citizen recently said that about 10% of folks from two local counties—just under 15,000 folks—got hydrocodone in 2014, according to Mike Stein, some behavioral health guy. Said they got 35,000 different scripts and maybe two million pills. That's enough for 560,000 days, for one person.

When these players spilled their guts, police learned that there was a $200 million pill business in the Dalton-Chattanooga area. The bad guys' sophistication improved post-Florida.

Imagine that.

Roughly 100 people participated in the North Georgia-Chattanooga pill mills, according to Jasper's dark research. And they're smart. They don't title personal possessions in their own names. Homes, cars, property, boats, airplanes are titled in someone else's name, someone too young to understand or too scared to squawk.

These criminals recruit prominent people in the legal field—top attorneys, judges, medical doctors, and any connected individual—with an opiate addiction. That sounds nuts, but then, one-out-of-ten citizens suffers from an opiate problem. Ask your doctor if opiate addiction is right for you!

It crosses all lines, all racial barriers, and all income levels. They hook up with these friends in high places, which helps when it comes to looking legitimate. Then they move away from cash-only transactions and accept insurance. This move requires supervising physicians—well-respected community doctors who supposedly self-regulate clinics by supervising medical care and staff.

Then the State of Georgia forced a requirement that physicians-in-good-standing must sign off as medical directors. Clinic owners fulfill that requirement by hiring pill-friendly docs, who not only accepted drugs, but receive a yearly salary to scribble their names on legal documents proclaiming them physicians-of-record.

Two such doctors in Georgia, like the one who ratted, drew a million dollars a year for this service, plus God-knows how many pills they swallowed for free.

Then pill shop owners dreamed up the buddy system.

Let's pretend you're my buddy, Mr. Stephens. The first month, I go in and receive my diabetes medicine. Or maybe it's for high blood pressure, toe fungus, hemorrhoids (gross), whatever. And you fill your opiate prescription.

Next month, we switch out. This takes twice as many people, but there are plenty of drug seekers and indigents out there trying to turn a buck. Teaming up addicts means the PMC looks more legitimate on paper.

Then Georgia officials started keeping a database of prescription pill users, just like Florida. After databases kicked in, the pill-scamming book-keepers traded customers' records with pill mill operators in other states—Tennessee, Alabama, North Carolina, Kentucky—which immediately watered down databases and confused pursuing law enforcement officials.

This creative practice kept pill-scamming patients clean because computers scanning databases never flagged them as doctor-shoppers. The folks running the databases didn't cross-reference with neighbor states then. So Billie-Bob Smith could show up in four states' files, get four times as many opiates as a sane man might need, and none would be the wiser to it.

Sneaky. But here's where Jasper and I think the genius of the make-it-look-legitimate plan came in. The Dalton PMC manager now-and-then faked MRI's, and then tipped off local authorities to arrest grifters—sponsors the Dalton manager didn't like, or wanted to eliminate from the system for personal or business reasons. He ratted out sacrificial lambs to provide his clinics with legitimacy in law enforcement circles, and with the general public.

As much as I hate these scumbags, I have to admire their craftiness, Mr. Stephens.

I'm only 18, I know, but before I held this particular knowledge of Leeza, her adopted family of sleaze balls, and the extent of the pill mills' reach, I thought the world was a simple place. Black and white. Good guys versus bad guys. Black hats, white hats.

That illusion poofed when Jasper and I dug into this thing. Now I see the complexity of human beings. It hurts my heart, and I grieve for mankind. But I'm glad I learned this early, before I motor off to college. It saved me a big old hurt down the road. I'm so open-hearted that I can't size people up right away.

Jasper possesses a wonderful intuition. He hangs out with folks a short time and figures them out, no matter how layered, shellacked, or full of bull they appear. Some people are born to smell a rat.

Jasper figured it out, but I'm learning.

Back to the bad guys.

When he realized the state had rolled out a database, the Dalton head-honcho-drug-manager enrolled in computer classes, asked around, studied manuals, taught himself to use electronic records and create fake charts with a single keystroke.

Auditors regularly scanned the books, and sometimes doubted a PMC's legitimacy. But over that four-year period, they never imagined a $200 million business flourished right under their noses.

These crooks fly under-the-radar effectively. I think that's why Leeza does so well locally.

After ratting out sponsors he didn't like, the Dalton manager moved clinics to quieter neighborhoods, built waiting rooms next door to keep lines of customers from view, and raked in more profits in deeper cover.

Formidable foes for Ed, Sarge, Jasper, and me—these pill-mill-masterminds. When I unloaded all this information on Sarge and Ed yesterday at Sunday dinner after church—thanks to Lois, who cooked a sugared ham for us—they were all quite impressed. Ed said Jasper and I might fit well into law enforcement careers, but I told him it was all there in the Chattanooga and Dalton newspapers. I just read and discovered and dug and persevered, and when I read how that bust went down, I applied that evidence to the local scene. Inserting Jasper into chatrooms confirmed my findings.

How did the Dalton gang get caught? I mentioned that the main guy ratted. But why?

Well, the FBI planted undercover patients, for one thing. That's how they learned the day-to-day.

Second, it was pure luck on the part of law enforcement. Sarge mentioned a similar scenario is brewing here in little Kituwah Falls as I'm scribbling in this journal. I'll keep this idea to myself for fear of hexing the whole takedown. I'm superstitious. Crossing my fingers. Knocking on wood. I always wear the same jersey to a Moto if I won the previous event. Keep wearing the same socks until I lose, too.

Stinky, but it works.

Bo Wruck's Journal

Before I get going, I want to thank you for asking Ms. Sullivan to teach me basic cooking outside of class. She's a sweetheart. Kids say she helps them fill out paperwork for college after hours, as well. Some folks teach because they love kids, I reckon. You don't do that job for the cash.

The weather is outstanding, Mr. Stephens, and I want to be out there on the dirt bike, but this journal, and a whole hour of study hall has to be got through before I'm free.

You keep asking me how we can rake in so much cash off the pills. I ought to be able to jot that down in an hour. I'm curious to know why you need so much information. You going to compete? Naw. You wouldn't look good covered in Louisville Slugger welts. Perhaps you want to slow or stop the pill business. Good luck with that.

I grew up seeing how all this works, and it's complicated, but I'll just spill it out in whatever order it falls. You can sort it out. We sell several kinds of pills, but most are opiates. Roxicodone, Oxycodone, Percocet, Vicodin, Lortab, Lorcet, and Tramadol. Most pill heads prefer roxy and oxy because they got no filler—no aspirin or Ibuprofen in them—which will ache your stomach.

Pain management clinics are the big key to our success. Crooked docs ask, "How is your pain, on a scale from one to ten?" If you say six or seven, they write a prescription for 160 oxies or roxies, plus some zanny bars on the side—we also call them footballs. If you say nine or ten, they hand over 240 oxies or roxies and 60 Xanax.

Guess what most people say their pain level is?

Back before 2010, when Big Pharma came out with a newfangled-oxy you can't crush to get a twelve-hour high in a single rush, either by snorting or mixing it with water and shooting it into your veins, the price was $80 for one 30mg pill. The good old days!

Since you can't crush them now, they lose that hit-you-all-at-once effect.

Sunny could tell you this drug stuff better than me. He should go become a chemist, or a pharmacist, but he can't sit still and concentrate that long.

Anyway, if you're seeking pills, you need an MRI. This big machine takes a picture of an area of your body, like a knee, a neck, a back. If you have an MRI with you when you visit the PMC, pills magically rain down on your little head.

Now, if you have a legitimate problem, an MRI comes with the territory. But if you're physically okay and just want drugs, you can buy an MRI off the street from a crooked person working at a hospital, a clinic, or from someone at home who's got access to some patient's old MRI pictures, plus a computer, scanner and printer.

The twisted doctors seeking cash are not real particular, though. You have an MRI that looks even close to legit, and you're good to go.

If you don't have an MRI, then we tell you to talk-good, look-good, and blab a good story. That works about 50% of the time with legit docs, and 100% of the time with crooked ones. They're ready to scribble on that pad when you hit the door.

Now some pill seekers have special arrangements with PMC doctors. Leeza and Lucinda just hired new physician assistants—women—and they don't go for that sort of thing. Oh, no. Cash only. But down in Florida, the PMC docs were sleaze bags, and they would accept sexual favors.

Hand them a *favor* and they scribble like maniacs on their little prescription pads.

Other docs will take drugs or cash under the table. We knew this one doc in Tampa who was a methadone junkie. Methadone's an opiate. These brilliant authorities get you off opiates with other opiates. That's good for business.

Makes you wonder where this ends, doesn't it? Open a shop down the street from the methadone clinic and sell Suboxone opiates to get you off methadone opiates. Then open another treatment center down the street from the Suboxone shop and repeat. Endless self-perpetuating capitalism. Mental and physical health ain't much concern. Gets in the way of money grabbing. Funeral directors got to order more caskets, more gas for frying drug-addled-carcasses. The money river flows on. Sounds damn harsh, if you look at it carefully.

But who does?

The methadone-junkie-doc can't write a script on himself. So his client base is made up of drug seekers, and he writes them up for 60 Percocets, and then he adds 30 methadone tabs for himself, which they swap out under the table. Everybody's happy!

The math:

You multiply 240 of those 30mg pills by $30 and get $7,200 street value.

The zannies go for a-dollar-a-milligram, and most of them are two milligrams. So if you sell your Xanax prescription, that's another $120. One trip to the doctor nets $7,320.

Now you know why these poor white folk don't work much anymore, either, because they lost their jobs to Mexicans, or to factories going overseas, and now they're addicted to pills, they're too lazy or think they're too dumb to go back to school and learn new skills to get technology jobs, but they love this pill business. Can't say what the black folks in Knoxville do, but I reckon it's the same. Turn the easy buck. Doesn't matter what your skin color is, or where your pappy's pappy came from.

Latino narcos and Middle East extremists dump heroin on America these days and folks drop like flies. More caskets! More gas! Good thing we're fracking that gas or we'd run out just from cremating opiate junkies.

Part of me mourns the opiate-dead. Lots of good-natured, talented people down the drain for no good reason. But another part of me says good riddance. If you can't act like a man and get over your little problems, then roll over and die. Pansy. Peeing in the gene pool is not acceptable.

That sounds cruel, and anti-business, I know. We can't sell pills to dead folks. But I just don't buy that tired old line that chomping pills or drowning in booze is a disease. Jeez. Give me a break. Lots of so-called scientists disagree, I know. They write those disease books and make a killing.

And some of them dry-out farms—like the Betty Ford Center—make a hundred grand every three months off rich folks who feel bad they got out of bed every morning and worked jobs, while little Jane and Johnny got smashed after school because nobody was looking after them.

Them dry-out-farms make nearly as much money as pill clinics, and they ain't going away, either. What a racket. When I retire from professional motocross racing, I'll leverage my cash and open a luxury, super-doper dry-out fat-farm resort. Rich junkies will sling cash at me over and over again, because why get around to figuring out the *real* reason they stay perpetually stoned? We'll call it a disease. Throw a towel over the mirror. Don't look!

Ka-ching.

Society demands the disease-angle, I reckon. Otherwise, we'd need to fix whatever sick things scurry around inside our heads. Ain't going to happen.

The way I look at it—if anyone should be an addict, it's me. Look at folks surrounding me: Leeza and Pussycat are juicers; Sean and Slowburn inhale weed. If you look up *Vicodin*, you see Bushrod's picture next to it. Sunny will eat, smoke, or drink anything at hand once the business day is over. They all live in Zombie Land. The Walking Dead of Kituwah Falls.

So if the folks closest to you are junkies, and your fraternal twin is an addict, then it stands to reason that you're genetically prone, eh?

But I'm not.

Can't say I've never tried it. Tried it *all* a couple of times. The high is okay, downright feels good at times, if the day is done and the work is over. But the next day is always a wash. And I want to be in the next day. The next day is important.

The high of winning a Moto is much better for me than stumbling around in a black fog. Crossing the finish line first. Nothing touches that. I like being straightedge. In this world, it's a real advantage.

I've always got the cool head when others around me crash and burn. The problem I face now is getting a *big* head. Which is easy to do when everyone around you is a drooling zombie with untied shoes, a stinky-brown stain on the butt of their jeans, and bits of uneaten food on their T-shirt.

Guess I got that in common with Sam and Jasper. We all came from common folk, and we're on our way to better things, better lives. So maybe it comes down to choice, and being able to see the big picture instead of the moment. Because if this thing were totally genetic, we'd all be junkies. Everyone has a junkie in the ancestor-closet, I reckon. Maybe Sam Walker ain't so pure, neither.

Well, don't I know that for a fact!

But I realize that being straightedge and being *good* at racing feels *great*. And winning; that's a high, too! I'm hoping to be on my own, with a real MX sponsor after high school. I can do it!

Most of our pill-mill sponsored users doctor-shop. Doctor-shopping is to the pill business what compound interest is to the banking business. They go to Kituwah Falls, Madisonville, Sweetwater, Maryville, Knoxville, Athens; these PMC's are all over East Tennessee, and there's no shortage of crooked docs and sleazy medical workers. Even dentists and dental assistants are players.

Once a sponsored user gets into the game, they can afford a car and gas. Most of them don't fool with insurance, and that's a requirement to drive in Tennessee. They sometimes get caught after smashing cars without holding insurance. We tell them to get some, but most don't listen. They're listening to the buzz in their little heads. Either that, or they *want* to go to jail and get three squares, a bed, and an excuse to dry out for a bit.

So let's look at our cut from one sponsored user, low-ball figures. After we pay them out, we pull between $5,000 and $6,000 per user per visit. If they visit just three doctors a month, we get at least $15,000 per user, gross.

I'm the collections guy. Some people try to run and forget where they got the money in the first place. When that happens, I get to ride my dirt bike or Jeep around the county collecting money, so I know that there's about 200 people a month using our Kituwah Falls PMC. I've got the list of names and addresses in my backpack. I know every back road in the county and the service roads in the forestland, as well.

So 200 people bringing in $15k each, times two clinics, makes us six mil a month. Of course, we have overhead—the building, utilities, payroll, all that. Got to pay off the local sheriff and his dumb-ass sidekick. But you can see it beats the heck out of dragging trees out of the forest and cutting lumber for a living, the way they sweated back in the day here in Kituwah Falls.

Plus, we get all the money raked off legitimate customers. We try to keep those plentiful, as it makes us appear legit. The day our pill mill smells fishy is the day the federal cats will eat us for lunch.

You'd have to ask Leeza about net profit, because she never spills the beans. All I know is I have the best Yamaha race bike money can buy, a 2014 Jeep Cherokee I use in bad weather, a Yamaha rice rocket street bike for enjoying the Cherohala, and a licensed XR250R Honda dirt bike for running down cheats when it ain't raining. Leeza hands over $500 a week spending money. Almost all of mine goes in the bank.

Who could spend all that?

Sunny could.

There are other ways to get pills. Some dealers avoid doctors altogether, and just buy scripts from poor locals with illegal drug habits; veterans, usually. Medicare or Medicaid patients, crack and heroin addicts. I've heard many in Knoxville are HIV patients.

Crack heads trade $80 worth of pills for $20 worth of crack. Gots to have that crack.

HIV folk are good for business because they pull regular scripts for opioids and anti-depressants, like Xanax. They trade pills for cash or illegal drugs. Most are broke and need the cash.

Veterans get meds through the VA, usually roxies, which they trade for heroin, weed, whatever.

We also pull pills from crooked medical workers. Inside connections. Sleaze balls working in PMC's, pharmacies, and dental clinics supply drugs and prescription pads stolen from work sites. They short legit patients when dispensing drugs; they tear off blank scripts, steal whole pads, and file false inventory claims.

They also alert dealers to shipment arrivals, and break into their employers' businesses after hours. They look the other way when false scripts come over the window. They're paid in cash, pills or sex.

Wonderful world, ain't it?

Doctors' kids are great sources, because their MD parents receive free samples from Big Pharma. There's a doctor's kid up in Sweetwater who sells to his high school. Wouldn't doubt it if he's elected class president. Zombie-in-Chief.

Medical insurance fraud, Medicare prescription fraud, and the MRI racket all count pretty big. Real MRI's cost $1,000 if they're legit, so shady employees sell copies for $200 a pop. They also steal real MRI's from car wreck patients, or back-pain patients.

Learned all that down in EZ-Dayz, America's Trailer Park. We simply refine the process up here, and our client list grows like honeysuckle on a hot spring night. Nothing like honeysuckle in your nostrils, winding through the sweepers cruising down the Cherohala. Sure beats that car-crowded, blue-smoke-hazy, flat ground, sizzling-old-fart-infested Florida. Love the mountains here!

How does it feel to have your manly parts in a vise, Mr. Stephens? I can crank down the handle any time. You know that, don't you?

And it feels good getting this all out, too. Win-win, for me.

There's the bell! Time to get out into the sunshine, out on my motorcycle, smell that air, and collect us some payments. Good for the lungs. Good for my racing career. Win-win.

For me.

Sarge Walker's Farmhouse

After Jasper picked up Sam, and the dust cleared from their dirt bike blast down the gravel driveway toward school, Sarge dialed the landline and spoke softly to Benjamin Nease, the accomplished only-son of his old-buddy from Special Operations in Vietnam.

Benjamin, inheriting the rough, good looks and identifying mannerisms of his father, was now a suit at the TBI in Chattanooga, in charge of methamphetamine and prescription drug abuse interdiction for Monroe County.

"What's up, Sarge?" asked Benjamin.

"I'm not sure how many more funerals I can attend before we act," Sarge replied.

"Reminds me of that crater story on the Ho Chi Minh Trail in Laos," said Benjamin. "If I remember the tale correctly, patience pays."

"This is worse," said Sarge. "I know these folks personally, people on both sides of the battle line."

"How's our man on the inside?" asked Nease. "I haven't heard from him in two weeks."

"The Wrucks sniffed him out," said Sarge. "I think he slipped up and his crooked deputy brother ratted him out to Leeza. Last we heard, Jesse ran off to Chicago to get lost in the masses," said Sarge. "I'm guessing he thinks Bushrod's too lazy to ferret him out. But Leeza won't let it rest, you can bet on it."

"Bushrod can't read a bus schedule," said Benjamin. "But then again, neither can Jesse. Do we need to place someone else inside Madisonville?"

"No. Leeza has Madisonville sealed up tight at this point. But they're about to implode over here in Kituwah Falls," said Sarge. "Knoxville is dealing with a loose cannon, gonna make the whole empire topple."

"Blankenship and Williams?" asked Benjamin.

"I'm praying," said Sarge. "I don't see how they can control Kituwah Falls much longer."

"Stand fast," said Benjamin. "Let them bunch up, and we'll corral the whole herd."

"Just like '68," said Sarge.

"Exactly," said Nease.

Laos, Ho Chi Minh Trail

First Lieutenant Coolidge Nease—Benjamin's father—hid beside the Ho Chi Minh Trail with eight other Special Ops soldiers that day in 1968, calling in coordinates for B-52 strikes against the NVA supply chain, which was coursing toward the south to resupply their comrades with tons of munitions, provisions, and reinforcements.

"The line is too strung out to take them on," whispered Sarge, lying prone next to Nease, greasepaint covering their faces, camouflage hiding them behind a pile of decaying trees.

"We'll bottle them up," whispered Nease.

The squad fell back 200 yards on the Lieutenant's silent arm signal and held a council-of-war beyond detection of the enemy.

After the platoon enjoyed a quick smoke, giving Nease time to gather his thoughts, he began. "Are there any tunnels in this stretch where the NVA can hide when we engage?"

"No, sir," came the reply. "We reconnoitered both ends of their present position yesterday after intel radioed their approach, and we checked down trail and spotted a B-52 daisy-cutter-crater south of this position, an hour from here at the half-step."

Nease peered at his boots, his mind swirling through the file cabinet of his mind. "Anyone recall the Siege of Petersburg, 1865?"

"Yes, sir," replied Sarge. "Virginia coal miners placed charges under the Confederate fort, behind entrenched lines, and after setting them off and killing 300 Rebels outright, a drunk Union officer ordered untrained soldiers into the crater, where they were slaughtered outright. Then another incompetent Union officer sent in a second wave."

"Nearly 4,000 Union casualties due to pure idiocy," said Nease, looking off into the jungle while shaking his head.

Forty-five minutes later, following a forced double-step-march—a moderate jog for Special Ops troops—the squad placed itself strategically around the crater.

The NVA, carrying supply loads, tramped 15 minutes behind.

Two Americans hid themselves off the north end of the 100-meter-wide, four-foot-deep crater. Two groups of three soldiers dispersed around each side of the hollow, and Nease and Sarge placed themselves on the southern edge. The jungle, thick and verdant around the hole, made the denuded crater a sure passage for the approaching NVA.

The Vietnamese force—uniformed veterans—would be formidable in an open firefight.

Vastly outnumbered, the Special Ops team relied on the element of surprise. Each man carried a grenade belt, an M76 machine gun, or a Winchester 1200 pump shotgun. None trusted the standard issue M16 in jungle humidity, and refused to carry the defective weapon on deep forays into enemy territory.

When the leading NVA soldier approached and stepped into the crater, the Special Ops team held fire. When this lead man reached the south end and the hole was filled with NVA from end-to-end, Sarge and Nease tossed grenades, then stood and poured fire onto the enemy. Special Ops soldiers on the north end stood and poured fire onto the trailing NVA, forcing remaining soldiers into the crater, while the flanking six dropped grenades and opened up.

When the smoke cleared, 83 NVA lay dead. Not a single Special Ops man fell that day. None wounded.

The assault fell deep into Laotian territory, out-of-bounds for US Forces. Therefore, the victory and body count was never transmitted to base, and the ten Army vets never spoke of it again in-country. They dug through unspoiled supplies and cached them in the jungle to leverage their remaining patrol stint. Some NVA carried diaries with pictures of their families and girlfriends enclosed.

***

TBI agent Benjamin Nease knew the tale because his dad leaked tears on a field trip to Petersburg, Virginia, when Ben was a high school freshman working on his US History merit badge, earning his way toward the Eagle Scout citation.

As they stood on the edge of the old Civil War crater, dad Coolidge recounted the Laos story.

On the long ride home, Coolidge whispered his wish that Benjamin never experience the horrors of combat.

But neither father nor son could predict the approaching drug war at the start of this new century, the worst kind of conflict—an Opiate Civil War—burning its own brand of pharmaceutical death, trauma, and spiritual darkness upon contemporary youth. Americans killing Americans.

And all for greed, easy cash, a seemingly effortless path to prosperity, a mindless escape from the rigors of living in a filthy-rich nation, silently abandoning its working class ethic to the scourge of doctor-prescribed dope.

Slowburn Wruck's Garage

Pussycat levered Bo's Yamaha up on the mechanic's-stand, preparing for the upcoming weekend race, the first of the new season. Bo had opted out of pre-season practice races. Alternately spitting tobacco juice and taking nips off a fifth of Buffalo Trace straight-bourbon-whiskey, Pussycat turned his head and spat a brown string of juice into the sunlit doorway.

Slowburn and Bushrod drove up, dismounted a new Dodge pickup, and entered the shop.

"Where you fellers been hiding out?" asked Pussycat.

"Been up to Madisonville tracking Jesse Davis," said Slowburn. "But he ain't there. So we drove back to town and chatted up his brother, Fred."

Pussycat spat another stream of Redman onto the floor and half his left foot.

"Fred said Jesse vamoosed to Chicago, some aunt's place up there," said Bushrod.

"Why would he do that?" asked Pussycat.

"He's working both sides," said Slowburn. He sat down on a shop stool, pulled out an old pouch of smoking tobacco, emptied and refilled with Tennessee Skunk and papers, and rolled himself a hog leg.

Bushrod stood fingering through a handful of pills, listening.

Firing the joint with an American flag-adorned Bic, Slowburn exhaled a bluish cloud and said, "Sandra Fogle told Leeza she saw Jesse talking to Ed and Sarge outside the Madisonville Clinic. Leeza tipped off Fred. When Fred asked Jesse, Little Brother couldn't fake the way his eyeballs expressed the blindsiding."

"Jesse never said anything outright," said Bushrod. "But last week, he lit out for Chicago, according to Fred."

"I'm surprised Fred'd rat out his own brother," said Pussycat.

"Fred?" said Slowburn. "Shit. He'd rat out his granny, if it meant saving his skin."

"I think I'll take a little vacation bus ride up to Chi-town," said Bushrod.

"Not yet. Maybe after we finish some business down here," said Slowburn.

Kituwah Falls High School

Bo Wruck stepped into the early afternoon sunshine, keyed the lock on the helmet hook, removed the brain bucket, pushed it onto his head, checked his backpack for essential ingredients, cinched the chin strap, fired up the XR250R, and headed west out of Kituwah Falls, up Jalapa Road, until he came to Levon Hill's residence, straddling the border of Monroe and McMinn Counties.

Levon, a long time KFPMC sponsor and distant kin to Lucinda, fell into deep arrears with the gang by forking chicken into his pot and percolating pills through his system.

Bo dismounted in the gravel driveway and slowly picked his way through abandoned clothes washers, defunct dryers, shelled-out car bodies, and uncountable bits of yard litter ranging in size from single cat turds to rusting rectangles of tin roofing sheets. He then knocked on the sprung door of a '60's era single-wide trailer, once a deep navy blue, but now faded periwinkle and dabbed in scabrous green mold, having been exposed to years of soap-less shade and relentless moisture. Bo heard hounds banging and bawling in the fenced backyard.

"Whatcha want?" yelled Levon from the couch, his shifting weight squinching rusty springs.

"You!" Bo yelled back into the darkness.

Levon appeared shirtless in overalls, the left strap dangling from his shoulder, a half-inch cigarette butt dangling from blackened lips. "Guess my time has come," he whispered.

"Bill's overdue," said Bo, pulling twelve-inch, tongue-and-groove Channelocks from his backpack.

"I gotta check coming in next week," said Levon.

"This will keep your memory fresh for that happy day," said Bo, pulling the door open and stepping inside.

He struck the old man on the right shoulder with the blunt side of the tool before opening its mouth, clamping down on Levon's bulbous nose, and twisting it back and forth, while Levon howled along with the chorus of hounds reacting to their master's screams for mercy.

Sarge Walker's Farmhouse

Sam rose early, showered, put on her school clothes and riding boots, thumped downstairs to the breakfast table, and began eating the cut apple, banana, fresh walnuts, and peanut butter Sarge set out for her when he heard her rustling upstairs.

When she finished the plate, she downed two glasses of water spiked with fresh lemon rose and peered out the kitchen window next to the refrigerator and said, "That's weird."

"What?" asked Sarge.

"Princess is crying and whining under your truck."

Sarge sat thinking for a minute, then said, "Stay inside."

He called the pooch, but she refused to come out, arching her back up against the driveshaft as Sarge bent down to look. He stood, pulled his phone from his chest pocket, and dialed Cornelius.

Five minutes later, the Whitlocks pulled up in their Jeep.

"Were you home all last night?" asked Cornelius.

"No," said Sarge. "Ed and I ate at a restaurant in Madisonville yesterday evening. Sam was out practicing for the Moto with Jasper, and she said y'all ate over at your house."

"That's right," said Cornelius. "Which vehicle did you take to the restaurant?"

"Rode our cruisers," replied Sarge. "Gorgeous weather yesterday. Ate at the Happy Jalapeno."

"Is the hood-lock inside the cab?" asked Cornelius.

"Yessir," said Sarge. "And the hood lever is in the middle of the grill."

Cornelius walked lightly up to the old Silverado, opened the driver's side door, found the hood latch, gently opened it, then stepped to the front of the vehicle and slowly lifted the hood after easing open the hood lever. He pulled a small crescent wrench from the tool pocket on the right leg of his overalls and unbolted the positive and negative cables from the battery. Then he carefully crawled under the truck as the dog fidgeted, whined, and squirmed.

"There it is, attached to the starter," said Cornelius.

"Sons-a-*bitches*," said Sarge.

Highlands Motocross Raceway, Madisonville

Sarge's brown Silverado pulled into the pits with the 14-foot toy-hauler behind, holding Samantha's CRF250R Honda and Cornelius's tools. The Whitlocks' Jeep tailed them, and when Sarge stopped in front of the Wrucks' outsized tent, Jasper and Cornelius looked on as Sam sat in the truck's shotgun seat and cringed at the thought of the coming conversation.

Pussycat, Bushrod, and Slowburn lazed in oversize lawn chairs beside Bo's Yamaha, which was resting on a low stand. Bo, already wearing his full leathers, appeared in the tent door with Leeza. Sunny and Sean weren't there, yet.

Sarge slowly opened the driver's-side door, got out, and walked up to the gang. "What do you think of this old pickup?" asked Sarge. "Sure looks good after all these years, don't you think?"

"Same piece of shit it's always been," said Slowburn.

"Fires right up, just like always," said Sarge.

Pussycat spit a long stream of tobacco juice that retreated to his right shirtsleeve after the main gob strung back from the grass.

After a long stare and a resigned sigh, Sarge said, "Now that you've showed your hand, we'll be taking you down shortly."

"What are you talking about?" asked Leeza.

"You'll have to ask these deviants," said Sarge. "But I reckon they won't own up to anything. That wouldn't be in their nature." He slowly spun on his heel, returned to his seat, fired up the Chevy, and drove slowly with Cornelius and Jasper in the rear-view-mirror as they all headed for their designated pit spot.

***

At 1:45pm, Sam lined up at the start with the other 32 competitors and looked directly to her left, where Bo sat on his silent bike, his helmet placed on the gas tank.

"What was Sarge talking about this morning?" asked Bo.

"Cornelius found C-4 wired to the Silverado's starter yesterday," said Sam. "That's pretty old school, like your man Pussycat—can't get past the Vietnam engineer thing. These days, assassins use magnetic bombs wired to brakes or accelerators."

Bo just looked at her in disbelief and shook his head.

"Maybe you've followed this crowd long enough," said Sam. "Unless you're aching to crash and burn, too."

Bo, flashing red in the face, forced the helmet down and lashed the strap to his chin. Five minutes later, his anger forced a restart, plus a one-lap penalty, and when the green flag fell a second time, Sam rocketed ahead, flashed into the first turn, and held off all challenges the rest of the Moto.

She carried the overall-winner-trophy home at the end of the day.

Bo finished next-to-last in points.

***

That evening, as they stared down a microwaved frozen-pizza-supper, the fraternal twins argued about Bo's ability to focus on the track.

"I'll show you some focus," said Bo.

The kitchen door flew open and they launched across the cement steps, falling to the dirt, punching. Bo quickly gained an advantage, forced his knees upon Sunny's shoulders, and fisted Sunny's head repeatedly.

Slowburn let Bo blacken Sunny's eyes before driving him off with a booted kick.

179

When the boys gained feet on shaky legs, Bo strode over to his street bike, fired it up, lashed on his helmet, and blasted off toward the Cherohala. Screaming through the mountain passes, he repeatedly crossed the centered yellow line, stormed the sweepers, and spewed gravel into a green abyss off the highway's edges.

***

Sunny climbed the stairs to his room and washed down five 50mg oxycodone with repeated slugs of Wild Turkey. Over the course of the next hour, he drank off half the bottle of the sweet liquor while planning revenge.

Sometime in the wee hours of Sunday morning, he rolled over on his back, puked and choked, and slowly drowned in his own vomit.

***

When Sarge arrived at sunrise with Ed and another EMT, he helped carry Sunny's body to the truck, turned to leave, but then forced himself to about-face and stare down Slowburn, who sat weeping on the front steps.

"Hang it up now. Please," said Sarge.

"I wish it was that easy," said Slowburn.

Sarge stood blinking through his own tears at Slowburn's tortured face for a long minute. "You need to think about the other boy," said Sarge.

"Bo packed his dirt bike and took off early this morning, after we found Sunny. We've no idea where he's gone," said Slowburn.

"I'll find him," said Sarge.

He returned to the ambulance, sat shotgun next to Ed, and slowly bounced down the county highway toward the Madisonville County Morgue, lights off, siren silent, his heart twisting in his chest.

Samantha Walker's Journal

So many thoughts and emotions.

Saturday started out with Sarge facing down the Wrucks over the car bomb, then I took the trophy when Bo false-started and couldn't catch me up, then Sunny died from an overdose.

Lord, have mercy.

Now Bo's gone, probably deep in the Cherokee National Forest.

Jasper and I are left at home to ourselves, and we know we have to attend school these last two weeks. But our grades are set, testing is over, graduation is two weeks out, and we can't look out the window much longer while the hunt is on for Bo.

On top of all this craziness, Jasper and I agreed to attend different universities. We made a final decision last week and announced it at Sunday lunch, an hour before we heard about Sunny.

Jasper accepted the UT scholarship for its strong engineering program, and I signed on with East Tennessee State, due to its in-state tuition, the $4,000 Hope scholarship, a second scholarship for high school valedictorian pre-med students, and 'cause it's eighth in the nation for rural medicine.

After living through this opiate scourge, and seeing what it's done to our collective health and well-being, that's the program I want to pursue.

The Big Guy needs more warriors.

Jasper and I have been so close for so long; we know our love is for real. But then again, we're 18.

And have never dated anyone else.

The last thing we want to do is get married early and then have second thoughts. That would be even more painful than our present miserable condition of wanting sex, but holding off by necessity. Watching him walk away to Knoxville will rip my heart out, I know.

Lord, more mercy, please.

But we're going to try taking on the world alone for the first four years, and if this love hangs tough, if this love is *for real*, then we'll know, and we'll stand beside each other forever, and repeat the vows and repopulate Kituwah Falls with little Walker-Whitlocks.

Right now, I'm about nuts.

Which is another reason we need to join the search for Bo. Sitting here is killing us.

Cherokee National Forest

Failing to successfully track Bo Sunday afternoon, the Walkers and Whitlocks conferred and agreed he was more fisherman than hunter. They'd scouted him at the Fin and Feather Club Shooting Range, and agreed he couldn't hit a stationary can at 30 yards with a rifle, much less a handgun. Smallmouth bass or brown trout would supply him when whatever he'd carried into the forest—jerky, probably—ran out.

They also knew his riding skills and the nimbleness of the XR250R Honda, so they figured he'd climb to a remote area near fishing streams. Carrying a rifle would be problematic, but a sectioned pole, line, and store-bought flies were easily stowed. A sleeping bag, ground tarp, rain slicker, and small frying pan were missing from the Wrucks' front porch, according to Slowburn, who agreed that Bo would fish for protein.

At 6am, they broke fast in the Walkers' kitchen, Sarge laying out fried eggs, bacon, grits, and hot coffee. Ed volunteered to stay behind and man the short-wave radio station on Sarge's desk, should communications prove necessary.

"He'll be on a ridgeline, with a good view in all directions. That's my guess," said Sarge.

"The abandoned lookout tower on Waucheesi Mountain," started Jasper.

"Is near the headwaters of Sixmile, Kirkland, Coker, and Shuler Creeks," finished Sam.

Whenever the same ideas cropped out of their minds simultaneously, Sam and Jasper just looked at each other with the recognition of a long-married couple.

"He'll have to descend on foot a few hundred feet to catch a fish," said Cornelius.

183

"Yes. And those waters are a bit warm for trout," said Sarge. "But the smallmouth are plentiful and hungry this time of year."

"Always hungry, like me," said Jasper.

Sarge led them into the backyard, and they circled up, grasped hands, and prayed for everyone's safety, including Bo's.

They mounted dirt bikes. Sarge and Cornelius packed .40-caliber pistols in the large left breast pockets of their identical Aerostich Falstaff riding jackets, but agreed to not pull them unless threatened with death.

Jasper carried a short-wave, hand-held transmitter that could bounce an AM signal off the spring stratus clouds above the ridgeline, back to Ed's desk station, and the search party packed camping-grade walkie-talkies with three-mile range.

Sam's light, waterproof, Henry .22 rifle disassembled and fit snugly into its butt, so all she had to do was pop off the buttpad, pull out the magazine, action, and barrel, and screw the parts together using the Leatherman tool she carried. The disassembled pieces fit into her backpack along with a quart of water, zip ties, iodine, and jerky, in case the day wore on. Sarge advised her to load the magazine with .22 shorts. The 29-grain snub-nose subsonic bullet fired as quietly as an air gun pellet, traveled 1,045 feet-per-second, remained accurate at 75 yards, and— lodging in muscle—would put Bo down without hurting him.

Much.

***

As they motored slowly up Old Furnace Road toward Smith Field Road, the mist cleared and the ancient Appalachians, sparkling wet and green in spring moisture, beckoned them ahead toward Bo, who probably wished to remain hidden in the primeval brush for as long as it took to formulate a plan to escape the steel-barred fate the rest of his family had chosen.

When the informal search party came to the fork of Smith Field Road and Fire Road 126c, the Whitlocks kept to the main path and the Walkers hung left onto the FR126c, the vise tightening, should intuition prove true.

Twenty minutes later, the families reunited on the ridgeline and dismounted at the abandoned lookout, collapsed long ago, but still affording remarkable views of the long-winding valleys created by tectonic folding eons ago, valleys stretching endlessly east into North Carolina and west into Tennessee.

Bo's camp, hidden under a hastily fashioned lean-to of pine boughs layered atop two small boulders, revealed an abandoned sleeping bag, kitchen utensils, a cold frying pan, an empty can of refried beans, and a re-sealable plastic bag with bits of jerky floating at its greasy bottom. The XR250R, covered with dead-brown branches, leaned against a short pine nearby.

"I reckon he's out chasing lunch," observed Sarge aloud. He spied boot prints heading southeast, but didn't mention them.

When Sam asked if she could take Shuler Creek, lying in that direction, he nodded. "Assemble the Henry first," he recommended.

Sarge took Cornelius and Jasper and ascended toward Kirkland Creek.

***

At 9:35, Samantha glimpsed a flash of yellow T-shirt between trees at the far creek side. She knelt quickly behind a 20-foot poplar, 40 yards behind the fisherman, his hearing impaired by the rushing stream.

A minute later, Bo stepped into plain sight upon a low boulder standing dry above the creek and whipped his fishing line in the mid-morning sun. A smallmouth struck, and Bo became fully engaged in the fight.

Sam flicked off the safety, took a long, deep breath, focused at the end of her exhalation, and squeezed the trigger.

Bo cried out, dropped the pole, grabbed his left buttock, and then spun around to sight the source of the attack.

But Sam remained hidden in the shade behind the tree while he circled in small steps around the boulder, peering into the woods. When she loosed the second round, penetrating Bo's right buttock—target symmetry achieved—he fell screaming into the cold, rushing creek.

Sam leaned the Henry against the poplar, un-shouldered her backpack, pulled out the rawhide, sprinted the distance, leaped into the stream, held Bo's head underwater with both hands until his fight flagged, then dragged him ashore by his wrists as he coughed and sputtered, cursed and wriggled.

Safely ashore, she flopped him onto his back as he cried out in pain, zip-tied his hands behind his back, flipped him onto his stomach, where she left him mercifully off his buttocks, then zip-tied his feet.

"How could you shoot me, I didn't even have a chance!" he screamed.

"Take me to court and I'll plead guilty," she said. "Guilty of popping a cheeky-ass chuckle-head in the ass-cheeks." She laughed. "For the purpose of preventing an illegal pill mill operation from destroying more citizens of Kituwah Falls."

Smiling at the prose, though ignorant of its literary designation, she retrieved her backpack, pulled out the walkie-talkie, and radioed Sarge their location. Lifting her finger off the talk button, she turned back to Bo.

"Carrying any of those oxycodones?" she asked.

Bo shook his head. "They don't agree with me."

"Lucky you," Sam said, stuffing her jacket into the backpack and placing it under his head for a pillow.

Then she walked up-stream, retrieved the fishing pole lodged between two rocks, and reeled in the worn-out bass. When it was safely unhooked and returned to the stream, she turned to Bo, loosed the six-inch blade of her Gerber knife and asked, "Do you want me to dig out those rounds?"

Bo whimpered, squirmed, cussed, and flopped while they waited for Jasper to radio Ed, Ed to call volunteer services, and the EMT truck to wind up the mountain road from Kituwah Falls, and stretcher-bearers to hike in to their location.

During the long wait, Bo asked, "Why'd you track me down?"

"The State Police didn't know where to look," said Sam.

"What do they have to do with anything?" asked Bo.

"Levon Hill stumbled into County Hospital last night, screaming in pain and sporting a wet-gangrenous hole where his nose used to be," said Sam. "And somehow, they didn't believe his story about accidentally tearing it off all by himself."

"They didn't call Buddy McCoy?" asked Bo.

"Jon Green, our family doctor, works the emergency room Tuesday nights," Sam said with a smile.

Sweetwater Pain Management Clinic

Harry and Lucinda sat at the head of a large conference table in the well-appointed back room of the new Sweetwater PMC, facing down 27 new employees, young and ambitious medical workers from the surrounding area, whom Harry hired for the singular purpose of raking in cash from the prescription drug trade.

"You were hired with the understanding of a common commitment," said Harry after the formal introductions of each individual around the table.

"And if you work closely with Lucinda and me, there is no limit to our potential," he continued. "We have the ability and capacity to out-serve and out-play our competition and welcome their customers into our fold. You were hired for your ability to do so."

After a significant pause, Lucinda spoke: "Any questions?"

Nothing but smiles greeted her from the white-clad audience.

"All right then," said Harry. "The doors open at 1pm. Going forward, we'll conduct business from 7am until 7pm, six days a week. Shifts will be twelve-hours on, 24 hours off. The schedule is on the wall behind me. We'll discuss vacation time in six months, providing that y'all pull your weight and we're deep in the black. Since I thoroughly vetted each of you, I have no doubt we'll succeed. You are dismissed. Go get 'em!"

Harry and Lucinda stood, smiled at their new tribe, and walked to the front of the clinic to check cash registers, pill stores, and prescription pads one more time before flinging the doors open to a brave new opioid world.

Marvin Hughes's Residence

Bushrod drove his Explorer up the gravel driveway to Marvin Hughes's singlewide, noting an unfamiliar car in the driveway and no dogs lounging in the yard, their usual cacophony replaced by chirping birds. He'd sniped Marvin's butt from a distance back in April due to the large Rottweilers Hughes kept prowling the property.

He checked the interspersed rounds in his handgun, a stainless steel Taurus "Judge" .45-caliber behemoth also accepting .410 shotgun shells. Bushrod habitually filled the first two chambers with buckshot and the remaining three with anti-personnel .45-caliber rounds, figuring that if adversaries were able to ambulate after the shotgun blasts, he'd finish them with the longer-range .45's. He said a silent prayer that none of this would be necessary with his old pal Marvin before he ambled up to the front door.

Wondering why a thick-steel model set in a metal frame had replaced the old, flimsy-sprung aluminum door, he knocked and took a step back on the rickety wooden steps.

Scratchy dog sounds and muffled whining from deep inside the trailer furrowed Bushrod's brow, and he drew his Taurus.

Marvin, recently returned from Monroe County Hospital with his buttocks professionally bandaged, failed once more to return the $350 seed money Pussycat extended while Marvin lay on his stomach in the hospital bed, whining for more opiates.

Angered over the forced visit to Marvin's, Bushrod began his morning with an extra-handful of Vicodin, washed down with the usual cat-head-biscuit-red-eye-gravy-buttery-hash-brown-black-coffee breakfast.

Feeling fuzzy on the way to Marvin's, Bushrod neglected to piece together the signs presenting themselves in the trailer yard as he stood cringing, hand-over-his-eyes in the mid-morning sun.

Twisting the knob, he felt the door swing inward, and he stepped inside yelling, "Marvin, you in here?"

Temporarily blinded by the dark interior, he heard the front door slam and lock behind him. Marvin's cousin Gregory, hidden behind his vehicle in the yard, snuck behind Bushrod after he'd entered the trailer.

Six young Rottweilers in the 90-pound range—freed from Marvin's bedroom—sprang single-file down the narrow hallway and leaped upon Bushrod.

All five rounds arching out the barrel of the Judge found dog flesh, but the sixth animal, unscathed, leaped at Bushrod's throat as Gregory, returning to the trailer from the back kitchen door, followed down the hallway and finished Bushrod with a Louisville Slugger.

Marvin, feeling better after a month recuperating with oxycodone, helped Gregory drag Bushrod's remains into the woods after subduing the remaining Rottweiler with a large raw round steak.

Rolling the drug-clinic-enforcer into a pre-dug six-foot grave, they spent the remainder of the day pouring gasoline onto the corpse until nothing remained, bone-and-gristle incinerating to ash. Then they refilled the grave with Rottweiler remains and kept roasting bodies until near dark.

Finished with the cremations, they re-filled the hole with dirt, then dragged the tire-less, rusty shell of a 1962 Ford Falcon over the spot with a log chain hooked to Bushrod's Explorer, which Gregory immediately drove to Atlanta and fenced for pennies-on-the-dollar to people with access to junk-yard titles.

After watching cousin Gregory motor off into the twilight, Marvin turned back to the grave and prayed over Bushrod and the dogs, sending them all to God without one thought of repentance.

Then Marvin returned to the house, fried-up and wolfed-down a supper of eggs and bacon, washed up, then called Lucinda Hornback to arrange sponsorship with the new Sweetwater Pain Management Clinic.

The Wrucks' Garage

After Bushrod failed to appear for three days, Leeza and Slowburn met with Pussycat in the well-outfitted motorcycle shop behind their brick colonial. At mid-morning, Pussycat—already deep into a fifth of Tullamore Dew—imagined the worst for his old buddy Bushrod.

"When's the last time you saw him?" asked Leeza.

"He headed out Monday morning after breakfast to visit Marvin Hughes," said Pussycat.

"Marvin's just healing up from his last reminder, and he stiffs us again?" asked Leeza.

"This don't feel right," said Slowburn. "Are the Hughes connected to the Walkers, Whitlocks or Ed Trent?"

"The Walkers or Whitlocks may lay a trap, but they won't use criminal trash for bait," said Leeza. "I'll get Buddy and Fred over there this afternoon."

"Andy and Barney gone bad," slurred Pussycat.

After the Wrucks drove off, Pussycat returned to sucking whiskey and tinkering with Bo's Yamaha YZ250F.

At 11:20, a wasp stung him on the ear and Pussycat crushed it with his bare fingers. Then he decided to spray nests hanging from dark corners in the ceiling opposite the large south-facing swinging doors. But when he picked up the wasp-killer, the jug felt empty, so he splashed a quart of gasoline into the thick-plastic-bug-sprayer, screwed down the handle, pumped in air until the handle stiffened, and annihilated the pests with a fine powerful stream, smiling as they dropped straight to the floor.

Returning to work on the motorcycle, he flicked on the light switch when a passing rain cloud blocked the sun, darkening his workspace.

One naked bulb sprinkled with gasoline, next to the wasp nests and unheeded during the spraying, popped after electricity heated its core, and when the exposed filament arced a blue flame into the oxygenated-mix of still air at the ceiling, an explosion concussed Pussycat against the motorcycle sitting high on its mechanic's stand.

Pussycat, stabbed in the chest by handlebars, fought to keep the machine upright, but his over-reaction pulled the motorcycle off its stand onto himself, cracking the back of his head on the cement floor in the fall.

By the time next-door-neighbors smelled smoke, eyeballed flames, and summoned the Monroe County Volunteer Fire Department, Pussycat lay burnt to a crisp under the gas-leaking motocross bike, pressing him fast to the shop floor like a lover too spent to rise.

Sarge Walker's Farm House

"Benjamin Nease, Tennessee Bureau of Investigation."

"Sarge Walker."

"Sounded like a long-distance call," said Nease.

"Chattanooga ain't that far, but I get the Muddy Water's reference," said Sarge.

"The blues is what keeps me going," said Nease. "Whatcha got?"

"Well, if you Google *Knoxville, Tennessee pain clinics*, you get 139,000 results in 0.85 seconds," said Sarge.

"How many actual clinics?" asked Nease. "I want to compare my number to yours."

"Yellow Pages lists 144," said Sarge.

"Correct," said Nease.

"How many does Blankenship control?" asked Sarge.

"Guess," said Nease.

"Let's see. Kituwah Falls, Madisonville, Fort Louden, Maryville, and Lenoir City. Five," said Sarge.

"She has two more in Knoxville proper," said Nease. "Seven total."

"Dang," said Sarge. "You were holding out on me."

"You've helped us a ton," said Nease. "And we now have a man inside both Kituwah and Madisonville."

"Two sponsors?" asked Sarge.

"One pigeon. A double player," said Nease.

"Wayne Fogle," said Sarge. "We've seen him frequent both joints."

"Actually, the FBI just signed off on the bust this morning," said Nease. "Jesse Davis squealed from Chicago, praying we'll come down on the ring before Bushrod arrives. And Wayne Fogle is taking revenge out on his ex-wife and avoiding more jail time by blabbing down here. So we're ready to roll. Word from above says Blankenship's empire falls Tuesday the 17th. We're backing up the FBI, but they'll perform the takedown, as it's now a federal case. Cubans included. The Feds will hit Florida and East Tennessee simultaneously."

"Why didn't you call?" asked Sarge.

"My hand was reaching for the phone when you rang," said Nease.

Kituwah Falls High School

Sam rose from her folding chair, slowly ascended the steps to the stage, stood before the podium, gazed out at the crowd, clenched and unclenched her fists, and tried to speak.

No words came.

The audience, growing restless as the minute hand swept around the huge Westclox above the stage, squirmed as angst grew palpable inside the gymnasium. Lois, sitting between Sarge and Ed, grabbed a hand on each side and squeezed.

Sam held the long-prepared valedictorian address in her right hand, took one last look at the opening lines, smashed it into a ball, turned, and tossed it to Jasper, sitting in the front row salutatorian's seat.

"Dear faculty, administration, school board members, parents, guests, and Class of 2016," she began. "I appreciate this opportunity to address you this morning, and to give thanks for all the work and love many of you poured into our education over the last 13 years. All the love and support we've received from our parents and guardians, neighbors and friends, and all the love and support graciously extended by our close community. Our father's fathers worked together in the fields, shops, and the timber business, and new residents attain our shared history the moment they put down roots in this area that is so blessed with natural beauty."

Jasper beamed.

"But we have more work to accomplish, more problems to face, more love to extend. This graduation today is only a beginning. I know we're not supposed to talk about this—the elephant in the room. But I've waited too long to address the issue. We've all waited too long."

The crowd stirred, administrators looked fretfully back and forth at each other, faculty frowned or smiled nervously. Mr. Stephens kneaded his dark-trousered knees with both hands while the graduating seniors leaned forward in unison.

"Early this spring, Jasper and I accepted the task of researching the opiate epidemic sweeping the nation, research requested by my grandfather, who has been surveilling local pain clinics along with ex-Sheriff Ed Trent, and friends at the TBI. Mr. Stephens, who counsels victims of drug abuse every day, also guided us. Here's what we found in the way of facts."

She gracelessly lifted her graduation gown, pulled a sheet from the back pocket of her jeans, unfolded the papers, and began to read.

"All of this information was compiled by the American Society of Addiction Medicine. ASAM.org is their web address. They say that in 2012, 259 million prescriptions were written for opioids, more than enough to give every American adult their own bottle of pills. In 2014, 467,000 adolescents were nonmedical users of prescription pain relievers, with 168,000 becoming addicted. People often share their unused pain relievers, unaware of the dangers of nonmedical opioid use. Most adolescents who misuse prescription pain relievers are given them for free by a friend or relative."

Sam visibly shook. Then she continued.

"This is what the ASAM found, folks. The prescribing rates for prescription opioids among adolescents and young adults nearly doubled from 1994 to 2007. Women were more likely to have chronic pain, be prescribed pain relievers, be given higher doses, and use them for longer times than men. Women may become dependent on prescription pain relievers more quickly than men. Between 1999 and 2010, 48,000 women died of prescription pain reliever overdoses."

She stopped and surveilled the audience, with some appearing bored, but others enraptured.

Jasper nodded, so she went on.

"That's 48,000 women, y'all. They perished. From something that was supposed to help them. Right? Prescription pain reliever overdose deaths among women increased more than 400% from 1999 to 2010, compared to an increase of 237% among men, according to the Tennessee Division of Alcohol and Drug Abuse Services. Their 2014 report says: 'In Tennessee, people who are educated, married, or successful with their careers are three times more likely to use prescription drugs than others, and thus to find themselves addicted.' You think you're too smart for this to happen to you?"

Sarge smiled at her as she looked over the crowd.

"I left out the information pertaining to heroin overdoses, which are skyrocketing due to the states cracking down on pain clinics. And the rising price of prescription opiates is making heroin the opiate of choice. The Mexican cartels and ISIS dump them onto our shores, and rural residents in record numbers inject this heroin and perish prematurely."

Sam turned and smiled at Mr. Stephens. When she turned back, the smile evaporated.

"These are only cold, hard numbers. Facts. Blah blah blah. Let's look at *actual* people—the friends and neighbors we've buried, just this school year. Dylan Dykes. Sidney Hollyfield. Glenda-Jane Jackson. Ashley Sizer. Sunny Wruck. Obituaries fail to mention opiates, alcohol, overdose, or death-by-drugs, and I beg forgiveness from anyone in the audience offended by my recollection of their passing. The deceased are loved by their families, by the community, and we don't want any more opioid death falling upon Kituwah Falls. Yet, we remain silent. We cry, bite lips, turn away, deny—but now it's time we look into the mirror. Darkly. All of us."

Someone in the audience coughed, but she could see that all eyes were on her.

"Which includes me, Jasper, Cornelius, Sarge, Ed, Lois, Mr. Stephens, every administrator and board member on this stage and all of you listening. We all turn our heads, have turned them for years, have looked the other way, decided not to get involved, decided to let it go to chance. But it's time to look in the mirror."

The color drained from Sam's face. She looked up at the ceiling, and released a silent prayer into the air.

"Most of you recall that last October, I was injured in a racing accident, breaking my collarbone."

Sarge and Ed looked at each other. Lois squeezed harder.

"I was taken to the hospital for examination and treatment, and Lortabs were prescribed for the pain. But when the prescription ran out, I bought another bottle. From Bo Wruck."

She heard gasps from the crowd, and a chuckle or two.

"The physical pain evaporated with the Lortabs, and I must admit I felt good with those opiates in my system. The mental pain of finishing my high school years, which I've loved; personal problems with Jasper that are nobody's business, the mental anguish of knowing we'd split up at the end of the year, perhaps forever; the spiritual pain of relying only on myself instead of handing it over to God. All of that and more zipped away when I downed those little pills."

She paused, but Sarge's eyes were like laser beams on her face.

"So I continued to use Lortabs through the first week of April. When Sarge told me Leeza Wruck was my biological mother, and I simultaneously realized Bo had possessed my soul with that bottle, well. Both facts caused the desire for opiates to grow. But I forced myself to look in the mirror, to look outside myself for help, and I received it."

She stood motionless for a full minute, looking down, then at the ceiling, tears streaming from her eyes.

"April was tough, and I would have taken the easy way out in a different environment, maybe, but I made it through withdrawal with the help of my family, and the Whitlocks, Mr. Trent, and Ms. Bailey. Sarge knew I had a problem, I wasn't acting like myself. He found the stash, and with his help and love, I broke free. He could have gone ballistic. He could have thrown me out of the house. But he chose to love me and stand by me instead. So I'm not standing here talking down to anyone. I know what opiates do to your head, your body, and your soul. I get it. Some folks claim methadone clinics and Suboxone treatments are the answer. I don't buy that line of logic. Using opiates to keep people from using opiates just doesn't ring true when viewed through the lens of common sense. It may seem fine viewed through the lens of profit, but profit at the expense of lives is not justified. Is never justified."

The room was silent.

"People overdose on methadone and Suboxone, which have become street drugs and agents of overdose during all these years of being overprescribed."

Lois nodded and pursed her lips while Sam lifted another notecard.

"According to a CDC report released in 2012, 'Methadone remains a drug that contributes disproportionately to the excessive number of opioid pain reliever overdoses and associated medical and societal costs.' The CDC goes on to say: 'Vital statistics data suggest that the opioid pain reliever (OPR) methadone is involved in one-third of OPR-related overdose deaths, but it accounts for only a few percent of OPR prescriptions.'

Let's look at this logically. No honest doctor would prescribe booze to an alcoholic patient in order to alleviate his or her alcoholism. The only logical motivation for such an act would be outright greed. Some blame the global market and the loss of jobs for the opioid epidemic. But there are thousands of jobs going unfilled for want of people educated enough to win those positions. Yes, we might have to go back to school and learn new skills, employable skills. Yes, we might have to get up early in the morning, work hard all day, and put money in the bank, instead of buying stuff we don't really need. The radio, the TV, and the internet constantly bleat the message that we need more stuff. And more stuff is obviously not the answer."

Her words traveled around the auditorium and echoed in emphasis.

"Where do we go from here? What do we do now? There is no easy solution, no panacea, no *pill* that cures all ills."

Someone chuckled.

"But my heart tells me three things. First, we need to look outside ourselves. I don't care if you're Christian, Hindu, Buddhist, Muslim, Cherokee, atheist or agnostic. But I do know that when it's all about yourself, when it's all about your personal satisfaction, your instant gratification, your selfish needs, well. Your ego is not your amigo. Ego is an acronym for Elbowing-God-Out."

Lois smiled broadly.

"Take that any way you like. Under the First Amendment, we're able to worship any God we please, or no God at all. The acronym is a metaphor for putting yourself first. Looking beyond ourselves to the greater good can only help. We live in a society that focuses on and favors the individual. But perhaps it is time to look beyond our personal needs and to extend the arm of love to our neighbors. For when we look outside ourselves, something strange happens. We begin to heal."

Now Sarge smiled, but then he straightened again.

"Second, we need to improve ourselves through education. The old jobs, the logging jobs, the manufacturing jobs, the coal jobs are not coming back. Politicians promising the return of those industries are simply pandering to voters. We have to re-educate ourselves and match new skills to new jobs available now, and to the jobs of the future, some we cannot even imagine, yet. Just ask people who used to build carburetors. Ask people who built 8-track tape players. TV's with cathode ray tubes. Film cameras. The list is endless."

She took a deep breath. Her heart was racing. Her forehead was dripping.

"Third, we need to suck it up and look at the root cause of drug addiction. This is the most painful thing, the look in the mirror, but we must look. Treating opiate addiction with more opiates is not the answer. For even in the odd times when this method works—some claim it does, usually people who will make a buck off of it—that method side-steps the root cause, and therefore the problem will return. Using opiates to cure opiate addiction is a popular remedy because it's easy. It's profitable. It pads the portfolio. Facing the root cause is painful. Time consuming. Frightening. Doesn't make money. It's expensive. Takes time and effort. Counseling helps. We need more dedicated counselors like Mr. Stephens. One counselor serving 350 students is simply ridiculous. It would be an impossible task to properly serve that many students if they were simply looking to enter universities, community colleges, military service, or technical schools.

Never mind that school counselors also address problems at home, alcoholism, drug abuse, spouse abuse, elder abuse, and more. If you struggle with addiction, or know someone struggling, I beg you to ask yourself what is the root cause?"

She looked around the huge room and saw so many faces staring at her, and maybe some doubted a girl her age knew what she was talking about.

"The answer may be ugly. Trauma in some form appears to be the link. It may be dad beats mom. It may be brother physically abuses sister. It may be mother is never home, she's always out drinking, running the roads with friends. It may be incest. It may be self-hatred. It may be a genetic link to substance abuse inflamed by trauma. It may be a negative home environment hidden from public view. The darkness stays in the cellar of our lives and we strive to whitewash our existence to the eyes of the world in social media. The root cause could be one of a thousand horrible possibilities. Maybe your grandmother died needlessly from incompetent medical care at the local hospital. Maybe your dad deployed to Iraq or Afghanistan during your formative years. And returned home wounded or maimed."

Samantha looked at the ceiling, bit her bottom lip, and then dropped her eyes to meet Sarge's, brimming with tears.

"Or in a box."

The assembled sat stone cold, silent.

"If we blame the drug itself—the weed, the methamphetamine, the alcohol, the oxycodone, the Lortabs, the Vicodin—then we are not addressing the root cause, and we automatically forfeit our lives, or the lives of our addicted family members. We're dead before we even get a chance to live. If we file out of this school today seeking to avoid our reflection in the dark glass, seeking to avoid the root cause at any cost—like our lost loved ones who are not sharing this graduation exercise today—if we think one more pill, one more swig, one more hit, one more toke, one more vape will make it okay. Well. We'll keep reading obituaries that say things like: *Passed away at home. Age 22. Age 35. Age three. Age 18.*"

She saw Sean Sizer wipe a tear from his eyes.

"I'm frightened to pick up the paper each morning."

Sarge nodded and looked down.

"I will dedicate my life to fighting this scourge, starting with an undergraduate degree in public health, and eventually, God willing, a medical doctor degree in rural medicine from East Tennessee State. That is my pledge to you. My prayer is that you will join me and continue the difficult work of looking in the mirror, digging up the root cause of your problem, seeking psychiatric help, if that's what you need, and never giving up."

Sam turned, walked to Jasper as he rose from his seat, hugged him in front of the entire cheering assembly, then turned to Mr. Stephens, her tears mixing with his as they wrapped their arms around each other and sobbed.

Then she took her seat next to Jasper as the principal rose with school board members to hand diplomas to the Class of 2016.

Epilogue

Marvin Hughes allowed Sheriff Buddy and Deputy Fred to search his homestead, but said he couldn't remember when he'd last laid eyes on Bushrod. Buddy's cuffs dangled suggestively as he turned over or tossed aside Marvin's personal belongings. But they stayed attached to Buddy's belt loop.

Two weeks later, Fred and Buddy were visited by TBI agent Benjamin Nease, but this time, the cuffs failed to remain attached to belt loops, as Buddy and Fred were arrested for their connection to the PMC fraud.

Slowburn buys weed from underpaid guards, and pays them a bonus to let him smoke undisturbed in a corner of the exercise yard. He knows who killed Bushrod. But maybe now, as the sun starts to descend on his pathetic life, it just doesn't count for much.

The Cubans, Ron, and Odessa and Buladeen boarded a private jet in Miami and flew to Cuba on special business visas, after receiving an alert from an informant inside the Tennessee State House. They spend considerable free time spreading US dollars among Cuban officials when not lounging around Ernesto's luxury villa five miles west of Santo Domingo.

Benjamin Nease, promoted from Intelligence Analyst to Special Agent Criminal Investigator, continues to dismantle opiate-driven pill mill operations in East Tennessee.

Ed declined appointment to Interim Monroe County Sheriff after Buddy McCoy's arrest, but persuaded Sarge Walker to fill the role until after the November elections, while Ed slipped into the Deputy slot.

Cornelius applied for his seventh patent, a super-plasticized micro-cement grout compound used to shore up the quickly eroding Fontana Dam.

Moved by Sam's graduation address, Reuben Stephens spent the summer of 2016 seeking psychiatric counseling and intensive physical therapy to beat his decades-long marijuana habit.

Leeza Wruck, following in Digger Byrum's footsteps, attempted suicide by hanging from the chandelier in her master bedroom with one of Slowburn's leather Harley belts. But the Chinese-manufactured fixture pulled out of the ceiling under her weight, and Sarge performed mouth-to-mouth resuscitation, saving her life after arriving in the EMT truck with Ed and crew. She awaits trial in the Monroe County Jail on the female floor, just above Buddy and Fred.

The State of Tennessee continues to crack down on illegal pill mill operations while funding research for the prevention of opiate addiction through East Tennessee State University, an institution currently seeking community support for the construction of methadone clinics throughout the Tri-Cities region, as long as they are not located next to the university.

Eleven Monroe County residents perished from opiate overdose during the PMC era, while an estimated $210 million of net profit flowed into Grand Cayman bank accounts.

High success-rate criminal defense attorneys from New York banked retainers for the late-October 2016 first-round trials.

Bo Wruck revealed the location of his secret journal during his initial interrogation by the TBI, after bargaining for immunity and sharing his knowledge of the pain clinic operation. His buttocks healed without complication, leaving one blue pinprick dimple in the dead center of each well-muscled *gluteus maximus*.

Samantha Walker and Jasper Whitlock telephone on Sunday evenings and rendezvous in Kituwah Falls during holidays. They struggle in social situations with members of the opposite sex, but maintain healthy relationships through campus Christian organizations and intramural sports. They burst into laughter at the sight of rabbits, and writhe in deep sleep under sweaty dreams of a shared future.

About the Author

Gene Scott, a retired English and reading teacher, was born and raised on the prairie of Western Illinois, and has lived in Tennessee for thirty years with his much better half, Lana.

Follow the blog at genescottbooks.com.

CPSIA information can be obtained
at www.ICGtesting.com
Printed in the USA
LVOW08s0527041017
551080LV00002B/2/P